Harley House

Fred Maddox

PNEUMA SPRINGS PUBLISHING UK

First Published in 2013 by:
Pneuma Springs Publishing

Harley House
Copyright © 2013 Fred Maddox
ISBN13: 9781782283133

Fred Maddox has asserted his right under the Copyright, Designs and Patents Act, 1988, to be identified as Author of this Work

British Library Cataloguing in Publication Data. A catalogue record for this book is available from the British Library.

Pneuma Springs Publishing
A Subsidiary of Pneuma Springs Ltd.
7 Groveherst Road, Dartford Kent, DA1 5JD.
E: admin@pneumasprings.co.uk
W: www.pneumasprings.co.uk

Foreword

Do you ever take a moment to think about this beautiful world in which we live, or do you take it for granted as most of us do? It is home not only to human beings, though most of us are apt to forget this, but also home to a mind boggling variety of weird and wonderful creatures of all shapes and sizes. There are many species being discovered every day, and no doubt there are many more yet to be discovered, so what right has man to arrogantly assume control of this world when there are creatures which have been around for millions of years before we arrived?

In the grand scheme of things, this planet of ours is an insignificant speck of dust floating around in a galaxy we call the Milky Way. This galaxy contains so many stars and planets, it is impossible to count them all. To put our galaxy into perspective. If each of these planets and stars were a grain of sand you would be able to fill a two pound bag, and the Milky Way is only one of millions of galaxies we know about.

Our little world is approximately 4.5 billion years old. If we were to condense those 4.5 billion years into a 24hr clock, the human race would not have made an appearance until two minutes before midnight, long after other creatures had begun to roam this planet.

We humans are by no means the biggest, strongest, or fastest of this world's species, but we arrogantly assume we have a superior thinking brain, and in our relatively short space of time on this planet we have asserted our authority. Unlike our fellow creatures though, who are content to live by the rules of Mother Nature, and who take floods, fire, and famine, and even death in their stride, we humans cannot cope with such adversities. Instead of accepting that Mother Nature knows best how to run our home, we continue to interfere with the natural progression of things, presuming we are masters of our own destiny. Despite great strides in science and technology though, there are many mysterious happenings occurring about us for which we have no answer.

The human is a complex creature. He goes careering off into space in a determined effort to make deep space his own, erecting flags on any planet or lump of rock he manages to land on, claiming it as his own, and yet he still has a lot to learn about his own world. If he was to concentrate as much energy into understanding his own planet and work hand in hand with Mother Nature, instead of slowly destroying his own home, the world may be a better place to live. The trouble is, man doesn't know as much about his own environment as he thinks he does.

I still ask the question. How many of us actually sit down and wonder about this beautiful planet we live on? Do you ponder about the mysterious and unexplained happenings which take place, almost on a daily basis?

There are those of us who tend to scoff at the thought of ghosts for example, but who are we to say there are no such things. People may have genuinely seen events which have happened in the past. Could it be a warp in the time barrier? Now what is this time barrier you ask? There are eminent scientists who subscribe to the theory that there are several time layers wrapped around the Earth like the layers that make up an onion, and these layers are supposedly held apart by barriers. One or more of these barriers from time to time may develop a weak point, allowing it to be crossed. This of course is only a theory; after all, time is the invention of man. Can we not see back in time when we look out into space? The further we probe into that infinite blackness filled with billions upon billions of planets, the further we are looking back in time.

Now what about that weird phenomenon we call fate for instance, which we talk about in a matter-of-fact way? We know what happens but don't know how or why. The question has to be asked. Who it will happen to? Who controls where and when it will happen? It certainly isn't us.

There are many more such mysterious happenings for which we have no answer, and I don't think we ever will. My advice is, don't even try. The journey of life is like being strapped into the seat of a roller coaster carriage and sent on its way. You will experience many exhilarating moments I am sure, and also experience many scary moments as you are lifted high and then plunged back down to reality. You may enjoy your journey or you may hate it, unfortunately you have no control over it. Once started on your way, you cannot get off until the operator decides you can and brings your journey to an end, which begs the question, *who is* the operator?

1

Think what you will about this extraordinary story I am about to tell you. Some will dismiss it as a complete fantasy. Others will ponder the possibility that it just may be true. Then there are those of you who will know the truth, because you will have already travelled along this very same path.

My name is Peter Grice, which is not my real name of course; I prefer to keep that piece of information to myself. I grew up in the Yorkshire town of Ballington, a typical northern community whose skyline in those days was dominated by towering pyramid shaped coal mine slag heaps and huge, square, red brick Victorian cotton mill buildings. It was an industrious little town. The coal mines working at full stretch with the never ending reciprocal motion of those giant wheels sitting atop huge gantries hauling tub after tub of coal gouged from the bowels of the earth, and its cotton mills churning out a never ending supply of cloth. The main street, which barely afforded room for the vehicles trying to negotiate its narrow highway, was lined with an endless variety of shops, which apart from a small Woolworths store and a branch of the Fifty Shilling tailors, all were locally owned. The march of the large supermarkets had not yet reached here. In those days the town was enjoying virtual full employment, but if you were ever to find yourself in this town with its grey stone buildings blackened by years of industrial pollution, you would wonder where the money was being spent.

I was just one of many children attending an ordinary school and receiving a standard education. I liked my school and never played truant as so many regularly did. The only times I was tempted, was when it was my class's turn for physical training. Oh how I hated those press-ups and the running jumps at the vaulting horse and not quite making it, and what good throwing a medicine ball at each other did was a mystery to me. I know I felt fit for nothing after each of these sessions, so how was that benefiting me? My theory was it did you more harm than good. Most of the kids got excited when every so often we would march across to the nearby park for a game of football, but I was hopeless at that as well. There was too much running around for me, but you had to play whether you liked it or not. I did complain to the teacher on one occasion that I didn't like football, to which he gave me a withering look and said, "Well you will just have to keep playing until you do like it." I wasn't bad at cricket though, but even then if I could get out of it I would.

Now after that description, you would think I would be a little round barrel of a child, but I was just the opposite. I was as thin as a rake with hardly any flesh on me at all. I am sure the teachers thought my parents were starving me, but it wasn't so. My mother was an excellent cook and saw to it I had well balanced meals, and that I was smartly dressed and polite. The one thing I did excel at was mathematics. Where others groaned at the thought of a maths lesson, I would literally look forward to it, and always came top of the class in that subject. I had a good head for figures. I took after my father in that respect. He had a well paid job as a wage and accounts clerk at a small paper mill on the edge of town. We were by no means a poor family, but we weren't rich either, we certainly didn't have money to throw about.

As with most towns, Ballington had its rough districts, like the Blackheath council estate which was controlled by the two Vernon brothers. It was a place you avoided unless it was absolutely necessary to go there.

On the opposite side of town was West Park, a very much upper class district full of large detached houses, wide tree lined avenues and two or three cars in the drive. This was where anyone who was anyone lived. I had dreamed for years, even as a boy, about being able to afford to buy a house at West Park.

Then there was the Larfield district where I lived. It was a pleasant enough area. The residents were decent friendly folk and I and my friends were free to roam its streets and parks without hassle, and as long as we didn't venture into the Vernon brother's territory there was no trouble, and generally we kept out of their way. They of course could go where they liked, and usually did. The only times we did clash was when the fair came to town. We weren't going to miss the fair, Vernon brothers or no Vernon brothers.

When it was time for me to leave school I thought I would struggle to find a decent job. Most of my friends headed for the coal mines, but there was no way I would be enticed to follow them, and the mills were even more of a no go area. My father though, being a typical forthright Yorkshire man, insisted that beggars couldn't be choosers, and now I had left school it was time for me to pay for my upkeep. One Saturday morning he told me he had found me a job at his friend's hardware store, and promptly marched me round there.

I was nothing but a general dogsbody, stacking shelves, making tea and running errands. As a young lad just left school I suppose it was to be expected, and although I hated the job I never took a day off and always did what was asked of me, but I was bored to tears knowing the job held no prospects. Then in a stroke of luck, a national household appliance retailer opened a big new store in town. I applied and got a job starting in the stores. Again I was the general dogsbody, running errands, making tea and so on, but this time the job had prospects. From day one I worked hard, did as I was told and never took time off. I was keen to impress. I had promotion in mind no matter how long it took. I did manage quite quickly to reach the post of assistant branch manager, but it was still a lowly position among the ranks of the company. It was a position in which you came under fire from both sides. You were the barrier between problem customers and the manager. You were also the barrier between the manager and the staff. In other words you took flak from both sides. Yes I did find it frustrating, I wanted to be the one to give orders not receive them. If I was to achieve my ambition though, it was a phase I was going to have to work through, although it was taking far too long as far as I was concerned. Eventually the Branch Manager retired and I was promoted in his place.

Even though I had achieved this position, it never went to my head. I was proud of my achievement of course, but never saw myself as anything but an ordinary man and treated my staff with the courtesy they deserved. I had always said that if we were all to have a short inscription of our character chiselled on our headstone such as 'Great achiever or 'Intrepid explorer' or 'Prolific inventor.' 'JUST AN ORDINARY MAN' are the words I would choose. Of course I would like to think perhaps my family and friends would want a more glowing description, but in all honesty this is what I was, an ordinary man, with ordinary looks leading an ordinary life and I believed that nothing would ever change that belief.

Now please don't get me wrong, I am not putting myself down, I think there is a lot to be said for being ordinary. Just imagine if you had managed to swim the channel in record time, or climbed the Himalayas, or sailed the Atlantic single handed. They would be no mean achievements, but it wouldn't stop there, would it? Human nature being what it is, your next achievement would have to be greater, like swimming the channel both ways non-stop, or climb Everest without oxygen and so on. The pressure to do ever more challenging feats would be enormous, so I thank my lucky stars that none of these were ever on my wish list. I wasn't driven by a desire to take on such undertakings. My view is, if people want to put their lives at risk, it was their prerogative. I suppose by their standards I would be considered to be a bit of a dullard, but I had my own priorities. I wanted to get on in life. I had goals to achieve, and as far as I was concerned I was no different than anyone else in that respect.

I was now married to Jane and we had produced two lovely children. I suppose we were classed as the average family, one boy and one girl. It wasn't planned that way though, it just happened. The eldest of the two, at 18 years of age, is James, who seems to be getting taller by the minute. I am no midget at just over 5' 11" but he was now on the point of overtaking me. He resembles me in some ways with his slightly sticky out ears, which I might add are hidden under a mass of dark wavy hair, which is also about to swallow the collar of his jacket. He has his mother's dark green eyes and slightly turned up nose. He is an intelligent lad (I like to think he gets his brains from his father) and we had high hopes he would go to college, but a job opportunity came up as an apprentice electrician, which he opted for.

Then there is Katherine, or Katy as she likes her friends to call her, although her mother doesn't share her enthusiasm for the shortened version. "You were christened Katherine not Katy," she would scold. "People should respect that." It never made any difference. "You might as well save your breath," I would repeatedly tell her. "She's coming on to seventeen-years-old with a mind of her own." Katherine was about to start college. She had hopes of becoming a Lawyer one day, and by the way she struts around informing us of her rights, I think she will make a good human rights lawyer. She is a pretty girl who features her mother very much, from that little turned up nose to the dimples in her cheeks, and with those beautiful green eyes she attracts plenty of attention from the boys. Most parents would worry about this, but she is more than capable of taking care of herself, in fact I pity the poor lad who she finally ensnares. She will be in charge of that relationship; I have no doubt about that.

Then of course there is Jane, my wonderful caring wife and mother. Standing at 5' 4" with a very slim but curvy figure, and long flowing natural blonde hair, she is the owner of those beautiful, tantalising green eyes the children have inherited, which was why I was attracted to her the very first time I saw her. When I looked into those hypnotic green eyes, I went weak at the knees. She could have been fat and ugly and bald, I wouldn't have noticed, I only saw those eyes, they had cast a spell over me. I could never figure out though what it was she saw in me all those years ago, but I wasn't going to spoil it by asking. She must have seen something in me, because we have been together now for almost 20 years.

We were both born in the Larfield district of Ballington. I suppose I would have to classify Larfield as an in between district. It had a mixture of both old and new, detached and semi-detached properties, most with squared off rear gardens and the obligatory Laburnum tree in the front garden. It was a pleasant enough place, but I still had that desire to one day be affluent enough to buy a property in Westpark.

"Why would you want to go and live in Westpark?" Jane would ask. "They are not our kind of people. They are just a bunch of snobs. I certainly don't want to live there; they are much nicer folk here in Larfield." Although I had this urge to live in a place like Westpark, I knew I would never be able to achieve it on a manager's salary, or even a regional manager's salary come to that, which was the next step up the ladder, but there was no harm in dreaming.

Ballington's industrial scene had changed steadily over the past few years. Two of the three coal mines had now closed and their slag heaps had been grassed over and trees planted. The cotton mills, as with most of Britain's industries, were suffering from cheaper imports. A couple of the mills had been re-invented as industrial estates churning out a variety of goods, but the rest had been abandoned by their owners and were now standing desolate and unloved and awaiting the fate of the bulldozers. On the other hand the town centre had been revamped, and now had a good mix of shops both local and national with a couple of cinemas thrown in. There were good road and rail links to most major cities and there was even a canal passing through the eastern fringes of the town. In my younger days I would join gangs of children queuing up at the double locks to help get the barges through.

Jane and I had met in Roosters, it was then the only disco in town. I was instantly smitten, although it wasn't quite the same for her. It took me six or seven tries to get her on a date. Jane was brought up by her Aunt Margaret. Both her parents had been killed in a road accident when Jane was very young, and her aunt had become very protective of her. I was given the wary eye by her each time I called on Jane, but eventually she could see I was very fond of her niece. Jane and I eventually married and set up home near to where we had lived as children, progressing later on to a nice detached three bedroom house on the edge of town.

As I have said we were a pretty average family with a pretty average outlook. I hasten to add we never considered ourselves boring of course. We celebrated birthdays and anniversaries and treated ourselves to meals out on special occasions and took nice holidays every year. We weren't into pot holing or rock climbing or windsurfing or anything as energetic as that. Jane and I just loved to stroll around our well stocked garden and, weather permitting, take nice long walks in the countryside.

I wasn't a person to think seriously about the unexplained mysteries of life. In fact I never thought about them at all. I took after my father for this point of view (he passed away shortly after Jane and I married, and mother two years later). If ever I was asked whether I thought there was life on other planets, I would shrug my shoulders and tell them I didn't really think about it. "They are too far away to bother us," I would say. "And if they had been visiting us in those imaginary flying saucers people kept seeing, they would soon scoot off again when they saw what a mess we were making of this planet." Then there are those who claim to have seen or even talked to ghosts or spirits of dead relatives or have been chased by a vampire. Come on, be serious, they have to be the product of an over active imagination. Has there ever been any concrete proof about such things? The answer to that question is, no there hasn't. By and large I was quite content to let other people get carried away with all the hype. Until someone came up with definite proof, as far as I was concerned it was all down to an overactive imagination.

Now, you may wonder why I am going to such pains to relate to you that ghosts ghouls and men from Mars had never figured whatsoever in my life. What I am trying to say is, if I was a person who had taken a keen interest and took to dabbling in the mysterious goings on which seem to surround us on a daily basis, I would have understood why I became the recipient of one of the strangest happenings I have ever experienced, but I wasn't that kind of person, so why did it happen to me? As it is, I still have mixed emotions about it all, but without doubt, the following a chain of events shook me to the core and made me take stock of what was going on around me.

2

I'll take you back to the January of 1975. Like most people after Christmas the bank balance was suffering from an overindulgence of the festive period and a bit of belt tightening was in force, except it didn't apply to Jane during the January sales.

We had enjoyed a lovely mild spell, particularly over the Christmas holiday period with everyone dressed in light summer clothing and taking tea on the patio, even the barbeques were out in force. The weather forecasters had predicted the unusual mild spell would last until the middle of February at least, but the British weather being notoriously unpredictable, and Mother Nature having other ideas about who is the boss, she naturally had the last word. Almost overnight, bitterly cold winds accompanied by rain and sleet swept the entire length of the country and kept it up for days on end. The world news seemed equally as miserable as the weather, with strikes aplenty and politics in disarray, there was really nothing to be cheerful about. Anyway enough of the doom and gloom, let's get on with the story.

I suppose it all started one Saturday morning, which up until then had been a pretty normal week both at home and at work. That particular morning in the Grice household had started like any other Saturday morning. The kids, not having to go to school, were as usual having their weekend lie-in, which enabled me to eat my breakfast in relative quiet as there was none of the chaos that usually accompanied breakfast time with the kids on school days. The peace would end though as soon as I reached the store. Saturdays, as you can imagine, is the busiest day of the week with the place full of potential buyers. I say potential, because there are plenty, who along with an army of screaming kids, stroll about the store with no intention of buying anything and keep the salesmen from the genuine customers by asking a million irrelevant questions while their kids run riot opening and shutting doors and twiddling knobs and covering everything in ice cream or chocolate or both with their sticky little fingers, and don't think it's just the kids from the grotty estates being little brats, oh no, the rich kids are just as revolting. After causing mayhem, they then casually walk out to visit another store to do a repeat performance. I have an idea it was the equivalent of a day at the seaside for some of them.

Normally I would not get home on a Saturday until about 7-30pm, which is why Jane was always up seeing I got off to work with a good breakfast inside me knowing I would most likely not have a decent meal all day. Then she would be off to her part time job at the local supermarket. We didn't need the money, although it came in handy, she just needed to get out of the house for a few hours and make friends and she enjoyed it.

There was nothing to indicate that this day was going to unleash the chain of events I am about to tell you about. It certainly started like any other Saturday, apart from the overcast sky and the occasional heavy sleety shower, the drive to work was routine. The traffic at this hour of a Saturday morning was always lighter than a weekday because most factories were closed and the shops hadn't yet opened their doors.

As I pulled into the store car park I could see some of the staff huddled under the canopy of the main entrance having their last fix of a cigarette before their coffee break. The previous Manager had never permitted them to stand smoking at the front entrance. If they wanted to smoke they would have to do so at the rear of the building out of sight. I wouldn't allow smoking in view of customers either, but as the store was not yet open I didn't bother enforcing that rule at this time of morning, to which of course they were only too ready to take advantage of my easy going nature. I didn't mind them smoking as long as they put them out before entering the premises. I wasn't a smoker, none of the family was, but I saw no reason to object to someone who did, as long as they didn't blow their smoke in my direction.

There was a yawned chorus of good mornings from the bleary eyed younger ones as they filed inside. They had, no doubt, been living it up in the dance halls or some nightclub until the early hours. They made their way to their workstations ready for the influx of customers. As was my usual routine on Saturday, I made for the general office to make a start on the weekly reports.

I had only been at my desk about an hour (Linda had just brought me a cup of coffee and a plate of my favourite ginger nut biscuits) when I was called to the sales desk. I took a good mouthful of my coffee before making my way to see what the problem was. My heart sank as I approached the sales desk. It was just my luck that the first customer of the day was an obnoxious baseball cap wearing lout who had been in the store twice in the week complaining about a television set he had purchased making crackling noises and spoiling his enjoyment. We had sent an engineer out to him on both occasions, but he could never find the fault. As the engineer had said, it could have been caused by passing vehicles or someone using old machinery, but this time apparently, the picture had gone altogether. He was ranting and raving in a raised voice and his face getting redder by the minute because he had missed his team's cup match being shown live. He was having none of my apologies and demanded the telephone number of head office. He threatened all sorts of action, including contacting 'The Trades Description people.' To calm him down I had to promise him a replacement set to be delivered as soon as possible, which he accepted, but he was still charged up about it, promising to phone head office to complain about selling him shoddy goods.

I returned to the office to my now cold coffee, hoping it wasn't going to be one of those days. In my experience when a day started like that it continued for the rest of the day, or week in some cases. Linda took pity on me and made me a nice fresh cup of coffee, knowing I liked to dunk my biscuits, and I continued with my reports.

After some time, I can't remember how long it was as I was engrossed in my paperwork, I looked up to see Tom Pearson the regional manager at the front desk in conversation with Colin the assistant manager, which was unusual in itself. For a start he rarely made an appearance on Saturdays, and when he did he would normally just bark a good morning and make straight to my office. The standard procedure would be to involve me in any conversations with the staff, so I wondered why he was talking to Colin without me there. In fact I have never known him not to do so. It was one company rule he had always insisted on.

I rose from my seat to see what was going on. As I did so he turned and headed his plump little body towards the office. I sat back down quickly and busied myself with the paperwork. The door opened and his fat little red face peered around the door. I looked up in surprise, pretending I hadn't seen him arrive.

"Good morning Mr Pearson," I said.

"Morning Peter," he replied curtly. "I would like to speak with you in your office."

You always get a feeling of impending doom when management does that. They do it with such a serious face, don't they? My immediate thought was that this mornings angry customer had contacted head office, and they in turn had sent the regional manager to sort it out. I was convinced I was in trouble for promising a new television set without authorisation from him and I was going to get a severe reprimand. Why else would he be here? It would have to be something serious for him to spoil his Saturday to come here. It could even be the sack I thought as we headed towards my office.

You never knew where you were with old Pearson. There were times when he insisted, quite strongly, that no decision was to be made without consulting him first. But when he was on holiday, or had to attend company meetings, he would say. "You are in charge while I'm away, Peter. I have complete trust in you to use your initiative." Which in my book is what the manager does? I often wished somebody would tell old Pearson that. It would be woe betide me on his return, if he thought I had made the wrong decision. I was thinking right now that this may be one of those times.

He made himself comfortable in my chair, and pointed to another chair situated at the other side of my desk. "Sit down, Peter."

My stomach turned. He never asked me to sit down, only when it was serious. His visits usually consisted of a tour of the store, where he insisted on tinkering with the displays, which we usually put back when he had gone. He would then make himself comfortable in my office with a cup of tea and go through the sales sheets.

I sank into the chair thinking of all sorts of reasons why he had insisted we talk in my office. He must have seen the anxious look on my face, but his expression never altered from his usual deadpan face. I think he took great delight in keeping his staff guessing.

"I've asked Mr Carson to take over your duties for a while. I don't want us to be disturbed?" There seemed to be the faintest of smiles across his face. I couldn't quite make out if he had a touch of wind or whether it was one of those gloating smiles. I swallowed hard and prepared myself for what was coming next, as Tom Pearson never smiled, gloatingly or otherwise. If he ever had, I must have been when I was on holiday. "How would you like a change of scenery?" he said.

I was now convinced that smile was a sadistic grin. My stomach turned over. I groaned to myself. "He's going to sack me. How on earth am I going to support my family?"

"I've been studying your performance on the shop floor," he continued. "And in particular the way you handle the customers." I knew it I thought. That horrible sod this morning has complained. "I must say I'm impressed, Peter," he continued. What did he say? Impressed? I was stunned for a moment. "Your paperwork is always neat and tidy and up to date, and your handling of the staff is very good."

I don't believe this I thought. Old Pearson praising me up? He's never done that all the while I've worked here. There has to be a but coming.

"I have to say, Peter, head office is delighted with your sales figures."

"Well I have a good team here," I replied trying to sound modest."

"What has impressed them most is your in store promotions. In fact they are so impressed by them they want to conduct national promotions with your ideas."

"That's fantastic," I replied. "I would be only too happy to throw a few ideas their way."

"They want more than that, Peter. They are going to create a new sales and promotional unit and they think you will be the ideal candidate to head the team. They will be advertising of course, that is the law I'm afraid, but between you and me the job is as good as yours. It also means moving to the head office at Garton. What do you think?"

I was taken aback. This news had knocked the wind out of my sails. Had I been offered a regional manager's job, I would have given an immediate yes, it would have been the next natural step, but this was a step in a completely different direction. What had thrown me more than anything was the praise for me coming from old Pearson. We hadn't exactly seen eye to eye during my term as manager. He wants to get rid of me I thought and this has presented him with the ideal opportunity.

"This has thrown me a bit," I said. "I was thinking my next move would be as regional manager."

"Forget Regional Manager, Peter. This shoots you three places up the ladder with a salary to match. If you are a success in this post, a directorship is the next step. If I was as good at figures as you I would apply for the position myself, but I know my limits. I can't say I'm not jealous of you, because I am, but I am certainly not going to stand in your way. I hope you will remember I said that when you are top of the tree."

He does want to get rid of me I thought. There is no way Tom Pearson would praise me like that if he didn't want me out of the way. He thinks I'm a threat to his job. Still it's a very lucrative offer, just think of the raise in my standard of living. The only drawback would be having to uproot my family and move them south, but I can't see them objecting to that with the kind of money I will be getting. Secretly I had already made the decision to accept the post. It was an opportunity I wasn't going to pass up, but I didn't want to sound too eager. "There's a lot to think about, Mr Pearson," I said.

"Of course there is, Peter, but you must realise it is an offer you would be foolish to refuse. It won't come your way again, or any other offer if it comes to that. If you turn it down, the company may well think you will not be prepared to ever leave Ballington. Think about it, Peter. Just think of the endless opportunities this move will bring about."

I knew what his game was, but I had to agree with what he was saying about being foolish to turn down this exciting opportunity. After all, promotion, especially on this scale, was what I had hoped and dreamed of. "I would love to take up the post," I enthused. "Obviously I will have to consult the family. We have a lot of friends here and my son has a job here. I would like to speak with them first."

"Of course you must speak with them," he replied. "But you will have to let me know not later than next Saturday, the management needs an answer. You will always have your job here if you decide not to take up the post, but as I have said, an opening like this may not present itself again, and if it does, I don't think it will be offered to you again. I will be sorry to lose you, Peter, but you have to grab these opportunities while you can. I'm sure you don't want to stay here as branch manager forever."

That night I gathered the family together to give them my exciting news, but it didn't go well. "I'm not leaving Ballington," growled James on hearing my news. "I've got a good job and lots of friends here."

"So have we all," I replied. "But I have been offered a good position in the company with good money. It will give us all a good lifestyle."

"I've got a good lifestyle here, Dad," He argued. "I have made some good friends here, and now you want me to leave them all and go to Garton. I don't think so."

"The same goes for me, Dad," interrupted Katherine. "I'm not going to Garton. It's miles away. Like James I have some good friends here and it's too far to come and see them. I'm settled here Dad. Why do you want to go and spoil things?"

"I know it's going to upset the routine for a while," I said. "But we will all make new friends and we will have a better lifestyle. I will be able to afford a bigger house in a nice area and a nice new car."

"We don't need a bigger house," grunted James. "I like this one. I want to stay here."

I was greatly disappointed by the children's reaction. I would have thought they would have jumped at the chance to improve their lot. I had to try and get Jane to talk them round. Now Jane is a very practical woman. Many times when there appeared to be a problem she would always come up with a sensible solution and the children always listened to her, but again I was in for a bitter disappointment.

"I'm sorry, Peter," she said. "I'm afraid I am with the children on this one."

I was speechless. I couldn't believe Jane wanted me to turn down this offer of a lifetime. "Are you telling me you don't want to move?" I asked.

She looked at me for a minute before answering. "We've lived in Ballington all our lives, Peter, and we have lived in this house for nearly twenty years. The children were born in this house and we have got it the way we want it. It is roomy and comfortable and in a nice area. We have all made nice friends and you have a good job with a decent income. We don't have money to throw about, but we are comfortable. Why would we want to move to a strange area and have to start all over again? I don't want to do it, Peter. I am too old to start all over again."

I was stunned. It was obvious she and the kids were determined not to make the move. "If I turn down this offer now," I said. "The company would take a dim view of it. They would think I wasn't interested in promotion and would never offer me the chance again."

"Let them think that," she replied. "Just tell them that you *are* interested in promotion, but not if it means uprooting your family."

"Companies don't work like that." I sighed. "If you want promotion you have to go where they send you. Besides it's a lot more money and a chance in the future of a directorship."

"That doesn't mean we are going to be happy, does it?"

I was getting very annoyed at this point. As far as I was concerned Jane was being very negative, which was unlike her. "Well, I've said yes now," I exploded.

"Then you had better go on your own then, hadn't you?"

That was it. I saw red. "If that is your attitude, I will. I am not going to turn down that kind of money."

"I hope it makes you very happy, Peter."

At this point Katherine intervened. "Now come on you two, let's have none of that kind of talk. Why don't you compromise?"

Jane and I stared at her for a moment "Compromise in what way?" asked Jane.

"Well, there's no guarantee you will like the job, is there dad? There is always that possibility it will not be all it's cracked up to be, then what will you do?" Jane and I looked at each other then to Katherine. "Here's my plan," she continued. "Tell your firm you will take the job. Then find a suitable place to rent in Garton for twelve months. Don't sell this place, James and myself will continue to live here and keep the place ticking over. You will know after twelve months whether you like your job or not or whether you are going to settle in Garton or not. If you don't, you have still got your house to come back to."

I thought it was a brilliant solution. It seemed Katherine was as good at problem solving as her mother. I breathed a sigh of relief when Jane agreed. I had no problem leaving the children to their own devices. Katherine had always been the independent one and James was a sensible lad with sensible friends, and it would also give him a bit of independence, so it made the plan all the more plausible. I wasted no time on Monday morning in informing Tom Pearson of my decision.

"You've earned it Peter," he said. "Under my guidance, you have been a good manager." I smiled to myself at that announcement. I thought he would have to take the praise for that, although to be fair I did pick up one or two useful tips from him. "I have no doubt you will be an asset to the company. I will be sorry to lose you, but I can't stand in the way of your progress."

I still couldn't get over this praise from old sour chops. He seemed a bit too pleased with my promotion for my liking. Perhaps I was right about him being glad to see the back of me, or was I being a bit unkind to him? Anyway, it didn't really matter. I was taking a big leap up the ladder which is what mattered most. Plus I would have the benefit of a bigger company car, plus the company had promised to pay all removal expenses once we had found ourselves a house there, and they very generously offered me a two week paid   holiday to allow me to settle in and arrange my affairs.

With that decision made, Jane and I wasted no time in making a visit to Garton to do a quick perusal of the place. The children didn't come with us. As neither were going to live there they had no interest in the place. Garton was about one hundred and twenty miles from Ballington. I had been there on several occasions when attending meetings at the head office. I didn't know the ins and outs of the town; I had never had the time to look around the place, but what I had seen I had liked the look of. It was a medium sized, affluent, market town set astride a broad but shallow river. Apart from a small light industrial complex on the edge of town, Garton was mainly a residential area with flower decked litter free tree lined streets and a good shopping centre which boasted of a good selection of well-known shops and a couple of small but beautifully tended parks. There were also a couple of cinemas, plenty of pubs, restaurants and café bars.

3

Jane and I spent most of our time travelling to and from Garton on house hunting expeditions. I think we had tried nearly every estate agent and visited nearly every area of the town. We had viewed at least a dozen properties, but as this was an affluent area, most of the rentals were far beyond what we were prepared to pay. The ones which were in our price range didn't have that 'this is the place for us' factor. I know we were initially only going to rent but it still had to be the right place. We did come across one property, which although didn't immediately strike us as being the ideal house, seemed like it might do for us temporarily. We would have liked to look at the inside, but it was now Saturday afternoon and the estate agents would not be open until Monday morning.

I decided, because it was such a beautiful day, I would deviate my route back to Ballington by taking a road which skirted a small reservoir. I intended to stop for a cup of coffee and a bite to eat at the café by the water's edge. As I was leaving the outskirts of Garton, we came across a detached bay windowed property standing in a good sized plot displaying a for rent sign. The gates of the drive were open so I drove in. A few knocks on the door brought the realisation that the property was empty. We did a quick scout around the rear, discovering that although the house looked in reasonable condition, the garden was in need of some loving care. We both took an instant liking to the place, but there was nothing we could do until Monday when the estate agents re-opened. I was excited to view the property inside.

Monday first thing, Jane and I returned to Garton. The estate agent told us the property had only just become vacant. Apparently the elderly lady who had lived there for quite a number of years had lost her husband, and she had now gone to live at the seaside with her sister. She didn't want to sell the place but was willing to rent it on short term leases, which fell in quite nicely with our plans.

Considering Garton was a much sought after area, the monthly rent was quite low. I reasoned it was because the lane fronting the house could be busy at times, especially during the rush hour as a lot of motorists used it as a short cut, plus the fact that the place needed a bit of D.I.Y. This was no problem to me as I was quite good when it came to a bit of renovation, and the traffic noise wouldn't bother us at all as it would only be certain times of the day. The most important and deciding factor though in our decision to rent this lovely old house, was that it had that homely feeling.

We quickly settled into our new place. It felt like home the day we moved in. You get that feeling with houses, don't you? You either feel comfortable with them or you don't. I had also settled into my job quite nicely, although Jane wasn't happy that I was spending more time there than at home. I explained, as with all new jobs you needed to spend the extra time familiarising yourself with the procedures, and as this was a new division within the company, all eyes were on it at the moment. I conceded it was especially demanding on my time but would eventually settle down. She became increasingly unhappy with the   situation though, and things became strained between us.

"You don't seem to care I am alone all day," she said during one our many tiffs. "And to make it worse you don't come home until very late some nights. It wouldn't be so bad if I had the children here to talk to, but I don't, and I haven't any friends I could go and have a cup of coffee with."

"You don't realise I have a very important job now," was my reply. "I don't get this sort of money being a nine to five man. If the directors choose to call meetings at night I cannot refuse. It goes with the job, you must understand that."

"All I know, Peter, is that I am stuck here twiddling my thumbs. If it is going to carry on like this, then I will go back to Ballington."

I sighed with frustration. Why couldn't she understand what my job entailed? Couldn't she see I was doing this to improve our life? I promised a few times I would try not to work late. I did mean what I had said at the time, but unfortunately it never seemed to work out that way and our arguments became more frequent. Then one night after I came in late yet again, it came to a head.

"I've had enough of this, Peter," announced Jane. "I am going back to Ballington. I feel as though I am being suffocated here."

"But you are getting to know some of the directors and their wives," I pleaded.

"Do you really think I want to be like them?" she snapped back. "All they talk about is how much money they have and how big a house they have and how many cruises they have been on."

"But we can go on these cruises now I am earning," I said. "We can match them any time." I knew as soon as I said it, that it was the wrong thing to say to Jane.

"Listen to yourself, Peter," she said. "You are becoming a snob just like they are. I don't want to be like them. I don't want to mix with them. They are not real people. Now you can either pack this job in and come with me, or you can stay here on your own."

"I can't leave just like that," I retorted. "Besides I like the job, and it's too good a job and too well paid to resign from. Things will improve just give it a bit more time."

The next evening when I returned home from work she had gone, leaving a note saying: 'I love you, Peter, but I can't live this way.'

Instead of feeling sad, I felt angry. Angry she had refused to see it my way, and I now looked on this as a battle of wills. I screwed up the note in anger and threw it away. "I've worked too hard to get this far," I told myself. "There is no way I am going to give it up now. She will come round, you'll see."

Unfortunately she didn't come round. Jane wasn't normally a stubborn woman, but she did have strong principles and knew what she wanted, whereas when it came to ultimatums, I could be as stubborn as a mule. We spoke on the phone frequently without ever reaching any agreement on the situation. At first I paid regular weekend visits to Ballington but they were increasingly turning out to be fruitless journeys. I never saw the children, because Katherine was now in college in the North, whilst James had always been out with his friends, and invariably, Jane and I ended up in an argument no matter how hard I tried not to. In the end it had come down to the odd phone call made by either one of us.

Whenever I could, I would take myself off for a nice relaxing scout around the area. The house was situated in a lovely location, surrounded by green fields and small wooded areas interwoven by narrow well-worn paths. Just over a mile down the lane, which at one time had served as one of the main coaching routes between York and London, stood The King's Arms, an old wooden beamed public house. It had at one time been an old coaching inn which had offered a change of horses for the coaches and refreshments for the passengers or even a bed for the night if desired. Apparently some King of that era had stopped overnight there, hence the name. Since Jane had left, on Sunday mornings I had grown into the habit of taking myself off for an exploratory walk to breathe in some fresh air and to blow the cobwebs away, and finally ending up at the Kings Arms for my Sunday lunch and a couple of pints of real ale.

It was during one of my walks, I discovered a different route to the Kings Arms via a narrow hedge lined path, which although added another fifteen minutes to the journey, was rather more pleasant than the direct route along the busy lane and having to bury myself into the hedge every time a vehicle came by. This new route took me past the rear of a large detached house. The first couple of times I didn't take much notice, but I began to get curious about the place. It appeared abandoned and looked to be very much in need of some loving care. Had Jane and I have known about this place when we were house hunting, we may have expressed an interest in it, although there wasn't an estate agents board displayed.

Being the curious sort, I stopped one day at the rusting double gates to give the place the once over. I noticed a plaque fixed to one of the gate posts which I suspect at one time had been highly polished brass, though now its surface was green and badly pitted making the inscription on it barely readable. On close inspection I could just make out the name Harley House inscribed on it. The place was sorely neglected with broken roof tiles, sagging moss filled guttering and paint peeled window frames, it was desperately in need of serious refurbishment. The garden, for want of a better description, was a large area of patchy unkempt grass bordered by weed choked flower beds and out of control shrubbery. At the top of a long pot holed moss covered asphalt drive, was a sizeable brick garage with large double doors, now rotting through lack of attention and secured with a hefty rusting lock and chain. Leaning against the garage was what appeared to be an old motorcycle, partly covered by a grubby tarpaulin sheet. I could just about make out a rusting wheel and a pair of handlebars poking out from under it. My heart skipped a beat as it looked very much like a Harley Davidson, but without seeing the rest of it up close I couldn't be sure. Harley Davidson motorcycles were a passion of mine in my younger days. I was the proud owner of a beautiful black and chrome Harley which I had named the cat because it purred. That was until you opened her up and then the roar was deafening. Mother used to be on edge whenever I went out on it until I came home again. Alas I had to part with my beautiful machine to pay for my wedding.

I stopped and stared up that drive every time I passed. I even brought my binoculars one day to try to make out what model that motorcycle was. I had thought about going to knock on the door and ask about it, but I never had the courage, and as there didn't seem to be anyone living there it would have been a fruitless task. I didn't like to just enter the garden without permission, it would be tantamount to trespassing. I certainly wouldn't want anyone entering my garden without permission.

One particular Sunday I stepped out of the door on what was to be my regular journey to the Kings Arms for Sunday lunch and my usual couple of pints. It was a gorgeous day with a beautiful blue sky and warm sunshine and the gentlest of breezes, so dressed in a short sleeved shirt and a pair of light khaki trousers; I sauntered steadily down the lane. I was looking forward to my Sunday pint, but at the same time I was in no hurry. With the warm sun on my face I was enjoying the stroll taking in the fresh air and listening to the birds chirping away, all competing with each other to have their songs heard.

As I drew level with the empty house, I heard the sound of a motorcycle engine being gently revved. I was taken completely by surprise; it was the first time I had heard any sign of life coming from the house. I peered over the hedge to see a dark haired, well-built man, sporting a short neatly trimmed beard and moustache. I would have said he was about 35 years of age and he was sitting astride that very same rusting machine which had been partly covered with that scruffy tarpaulin, only now, that machine wasn't rusty. I stared hard at it to make sure it was the same motorcycle, but there was no doubt it was by the number plate. That rusting pile, which had been partly hidden under the tarpaulin, was now a gleaming black and chrome super bike in showroom condition. It immediately brought back memories of the Harley Davidson I once owned. I stood rooted to the spot, I couldn't believe the transformation. Then I noticed the garage doors were wide open giving me a clear view of the interior. I stared in amazement at the array of motorcycles lined up inside. From what I could see they all appeared to be Harley Davidsons and in perfect condition and beautifully polished along with other machines in various stages of repair, but all meticulously clean.

I was so interested in the motorcycles, I wasn't aware the man had noticed me peering over the hedge. He sat and gazed at me for a moment while continuing to gently rev up the engine of the Harley. It wasn't a harsh stare, you know, a glare or anything. It was more like a stare of curiosity as much as to say who are you? What are you doing there? I was suddenly aware his eyes were on me. I felt as though I had invaded his privacy, so I thought I had better be on my way. I was just about to leave when he smiled and waved. I returned the acknowledgement.

The one thing I did notice, was that he kept glancing nervously at the sky. I looked up to see what had caught his attention. To my surprise a large black cloud had appeared on its own out of nowhere. I thought it strange as there were no clouds at all to be seen when I had started out, the sky had been absolutely clear. I didn't pay much heed to it, but as I was about to introduce myself, a blinding flash of lightning ripped across the sky. I instinctively ducked behind the hedge, as if that would protect me. It was over in a couple of seconds of course, but as I recovered I could hear the man crying out in terror. I straightened up to see he had fallen from his Harley and he was lying curled up in a bunch screaming "NO! NO!" I raced around to the gate and rushed to his side.

"What is it?" I asked. "Are you hurt?"

He slowly unfurled his hands from around his face and looked about him. He scrambled to his feet, again looking about him as he did so. I could see he was visibly shaken but apart from his ashen face, he appeared to be ok.

"What is it?" I asked again. "Is there anything I can do?"

He didn't answer and hurried toward the house, beckoning me to follow. The door led straight into the kitchen. I was a little taken aback at what greeted me. The dilapidated exterior gave no indication as to what was inside. I wiped my feet on the doormat which had seen better days and entered the kitchen. He was already seated at a large well scrubbed pine table in the middle of what was an old fashioned but bright clean kitchen. The red quarry tiled floor was spotless and an open coal fire was burning merrily away in an old fashioned iron grate giving out welcoming warmth.

"You need a stiff drink" I said. "Got any Brandy or Whisky anywhere?"

"I don't touch the stuff," he almost protested.

"What about a nice cup of tea?" I asked.

"No, nothing thanks. I'm ok now."

I pulled out one of the chairs and sat at the table. He held out his hand to shake mine and introduced himself as Greg Baker. "Pleased to meet you Greg," I replied. "I'm Peter Grice. I live in the detached place just up the lane from here."

He nodded. "Yes I know. I've seen you about."

Although I was extremely curious, I decided I wasn't going to embarrass him by asking what his problem was, but he knew I must have been curious at his actions. He looked at me several times as if to say something then lowered his eyes, he had obviously had a change of mind of what he wanted to tell me. I quickly changed the subject. "I always though this place was empty," I said looking around. "I've passed it many times but I've never seen anyone about."

"Yes," he replied softly. "It's left like this for a purpose." He could see me giving him a strange look. "I had better explain, Peter. I have been away for a while and I don't want anyone to know I am back here. I know that sounds strange, but I don't want people bothering me. I just want to be left in peace."

"Aren't you taking a chance repairing your bikes in the garden?" I asked. "Someone might see you."

"There are no more houses around here except yours," he replied. "You are the only person who ever comes this way."

I felt a bit guilty at that statement and apologised for disturbing him and suggested I go and leave him in peace. "No please don't go," he said. "I would like you to stay. You can come here as much as you like, but I would ask you to promise not to tell anyone I am here."

I was about to ask why that was but I thought better of it. This man, for reasons known only to him, wanted his privacy and I respected that. "You have my word on that, Greg."

"That's great," he said. "Perhaps you would like to give me a hand with my motorbikes."

"I'd love to," I said. "I couldn't help noticing them in the workshop. Are they all Harley's?"

"Yes," he replied. I have eight of them."

With the topic suddenly turning to motorcycles, the thunderstorm incident was forgotten for now. Needless to say, I never did make it to the Kings Arms that day. Greg and I became good friends over the next month, and although I never mentioned it to him again, I thought about the lighting incident quite often. I was still rather curious to know more about it and why it had such a traumatic effect on him.

4

I had now taken to strolling over to Greg's every Sunday to help with the renovation of his Harleys. It had become the highlight of my week and I was enjoying it immensely. It reminded me of my youth tinkering and polishing that Harley of mine and I suspect Greg was also enjoying the company.

It was one Sunday morning during a much needed break that Greg, suddenly out of the blue, blurted out. "You must think I'm a wimp being frightened of a bit of lightning."

I looked at him quizzically for a brief moment wondering what had made him suddenly come out with that statement. "I don't think anything of the kind," I assured him. "I hadn't thought any more about it." Which to be truthful, I hadn't. "We all have our little phobias," I said. "I'm scared to death of spiders myself. I can't even be in the same room as them."

"It's not a phobia exactly," he said. "I never used to be frightened of storms. It's what one may do that scares me."

I just stared at him blankly, I couldn't begin to think what he meant by that. He could see the confusion on my face and stared back at me for a minute. There was tension in his face and his mouth opened and shut as if to blurt something out, he then took an enormous sigh and fell silent. I got the impression, that for the second time, he was about to tell me something before having a change of heart.

"You don't have to explain anything to me, Greg." I assured him, trying to relieve his tension.

He thought for a moment. "I think the time has come to take you into my confidence, Peter. I have been looking for someone who I can have complete trust in, and now I think the time is right. My instincts tell me I can trust you to have an open mind."

That statement initially filled me with dread. "Don't tell me any of your innermost family secrets, Greg. If its tax evasion or you are hiding from the law, or anything like that, I don't want to know if you don't mind."

He shook his head. "It's nothing like that. I wish it was that simple."

I looked at him somewhat sympathetically. "Well I can see you need to get something off your chest. If it is going to make you feel better I am willing to listen. Shall we put the bikes away then you can tell me all about it."

He shook his head "Not today, Peter. There are four of us involved in this. If you are willing, and if the others agree, I'd like to get everyone together and we can all tell you what happened."

"Are you sure about this, Greg?" I said looking him full in the eyes. "After all you haven't known me that long."

"Long enough I think Peter. Long enough to know I can trust you."

I reluctantly agreed, and I say reluctantly because I really didn't want to be burdened with other people's secrets. I hated knowing someone else's business and having to keep it to myself. I always felt very awkward about it. I would sooner not know, but how could I refuse? Greg was obviously bursting to tell me, and seemed more than relieved he had found someone to confide in, plus I was flattered he trusted me enough to take me into his confidence.

The topic was once again suddenly switched to the motorcycles. It was as though we had never had the previous conversation. Greg had returned to his normal self and nothing more was said on the subject, both of us carried on where we left off with the job in hand.

That Sunday's incident played on my mind. I found myself thinking about it instead of concentrating on my work. I couldn't help wondering what it was all about. Who were these other people he had mentioned, and when was I going to meet them, and why the big secret? Many things flashed through my mind. I hoped and prayed I was not going to have to listen to, or be involved in something illegal. There was one thing I was certain of, that lightning bolt had something to do with it.

I hadn't time to think about Greg and his friends the following week. Easter weekend was fast approaching and I was concentrating on putting the finishing touches to a big Easter promotion which was to operate over the weekend. Plus I had to make sure all regional managers were up to speed with the campaign.

The Friday and Saturday, at head office could only be described as a madhouse due to the massive promotion we had advertised. As it happened, all my hard work had paid off. It turned out to be a record breaking two days and was a great start for my new position. The management were over the moon with my handling of the sales and the resulting profitability. It was very pleasing to me of course, because there would be a handsome bonus in it for me.

I must confess at this point I was missing Jane. I had worked hard to reach this position in the company and was earning the sort of money I could only dream about a few years ago. I admit the job had demanded more of my time, but it was no more than I had expected of someone in my position. Why Jane was so negative about that was beyond me. Didn't she want me to better myself? Surely she could see that life would now be more comfortable. I could understand the children not wanting to uproot themselves. James had a good job and had a good crowd of friends around him. Young people of that age are very reluctant to change their lifestyle. Katherine of course was her own person and had now started college anyway. As for Jane, I would have thought she would have been a bit more mature about all this. After all, as my wife, I had expected a bit more loyalty from her. I would have stood by her had the roles been reversed. However, I had made up my mind I was not going to give up my job and return to my old managerial position at the Ballington store as she wanted. I would be a fool to do so. For now the situation remained a stalemate and there was nothing I could do about it only play the waiting game.

I reached home late on that Saturday night completely exhausted. I had been thinking about popping down to the Kings Arms for a refreshing couple of drinks, but by the time I had prepared and eaten my meal I was too tired to go anywhere and just fell into bed. The next thing I knew it was Sunday morning. After breakfast and a quick tidy up I set off for my leisurely stroll to see Greg. I couldn't believe how the weather was holding up. I was greeted by yet another pleasant warm day, so dressed in a short sleeved shirt and a pair of light trousers and clutching a small Holdall containing a pair of overalls and a flask of coffee, I set off. This little stroll and stripping down those Harleys had become an unmissable pleasure for me. I must say that during my frequent excursions along this quiet little path, I had never encountered anyone else, which I suppose didn't really surprise me that much as the path ended at the house and then continued along a stretch of potholed dirt road leading from the house to a narrow country lane. I was never sure if that dirt road was private property or not, but no one had ever stopped me, so until they did, I would continue to use it.

As I have said, I always enjoyed my stroll to Greg's taking in the fresh clean air and listening to the chattering birds, but today for some reason, I had reached the house without recollection of the walk, which I put down to having other things on my mind.

I arrived at the house at the usual time to find it deathly quiet. There was no Greg tinkering with his bikes in the drive. The garage doors were locked,

28

and the place looked like the first day I discovered it. I stood at the gate looking towards the house and thinking he must have gone away for the weekend. I was sure he hadn't mentioned anything about a holiday. I was about to turn and head for the Kings Arms when for some reason I suddenly thought about the lightning incident, and although there hadn't been a recurrence of that event, I reminded myself he was on his own and may be in need of help again. I decided to give a knock on the door just to be sure he wasn't in there needing assistance. I made my way along the drive to the front door and pressed the bell. There was silence. I pressed it harder this time and cocked my ear to the door to listen for the chime, but still there was silence. It didn't surprise me at all that the bell push didn't work. It probably hadn't done so for some time. I decided to take a look around the rear of the house. I was about to knock on the kitchen door when it suddenly opened and there stood Greg.

He ushered me inside. "Come and meet the lads," he said. He led me through to a large pleasantly decorated room where a fire was blazing away in a cast iron log burner. The room was in semi darkness due to a pair of thin curtains drawn across the window allowing in only a faint glow of light with the log burner helping out the best it could. I was completely taken by surprise. I hadn't expected his friends to be here. There were no vehicles parked about so I assumed, like me, they all lived near enough to walk to the house.

"Grab a seat," he said pointing to a semicircle of armchairs arranged around the stove. We'll make ourselves comfortable. Then I will make the introductions."

They all settled back into their easy chairs. Greg looked about the room. He indicated to me. "This is Peter everybody. I will introduce each of you in turn." He pointed to a small man to my immediate right. He was I would say about 5' 8," of stout build with a slight pot belly. The top of his head was completely bald, but there was a thick border of dark hair extending from just above the ears and covering the nape of his neck to his collar. He had smiling blue eyes set in a rounded face. I noticed both his hands and face displayed several small faint blue scars made more visible because of his very pale skin. I learned at a later date that the scars were a result of coal dust penetrating into cuts sustained in his job as a coal miner. I guessed his age to be in the late forties early fifties. "This is Bill." We both shook hands. Greg then pointed to a tall, lean young man, who I thought to be in his late twenties and over 6 feet tall at a guess. His head was covered by an unkempt mass of blonde curls that stretched almost to shoulder length. He gazed at me with a pair of deep blue penetrating eyes and smiled. "This is Jason." Jason extended his hand in greeting. "And finally, next to him is Rod."

29

Rod was about the same height as me 5' 11" a bit on the stocky side but by no means overweight. I suppose you could have described him as muscular. He had a lightly tanned skin, though whether this was natural or the result of a tanning machine, I wouldn't like to say. He had an expertly styled head of jet black hair and also sported a small but equally neat moustache, and from underneath a pair of black neatly trimmed eyebrows peered a pair of large dark brown eyes. I shook hands with him and settled back in my chair.

Greg again looked around the half circle of chairs. "First I want to make sure we are all in agreement to tell our story to Peter. I assume we are or you wouldn't be here, but if you have had a change of mind speak now." The room was quiet for a moment as they looked at each other in turn.

"You know Peter better than anyone here, Greg," voiced Bill. "If you vouch for him that is good enough for me." The rest of them nodded agreement to that statement.

Greg pointed to me. "If I didn't trust this man I wouldn't be prepared to tell him our experience. The most important thing for you to know, is that Peter will have an open mind about what we have to tell him." Greg looked me in the eye. "You see, Peter, it is imperative to us that you sincerely believe what we have to tell you. There may come a time when you will want to relate our experience, but for now though, it is vital we have your assurance that what we are about to tell you will go no further than this room."

"I can assure you of an open mind, Greg." I said. "And you have my guarantee that what you are about to say will go no further than these four walls."

I settled back in my chair eager to hear this mysterious story. Greg leaned forward and looked me in the eye. "It's difficult to know where to start. As you can see there are four of us involved. Each of us trod a different path to our experience, so we all have a different story to tell, and I must tell you this. We are not the same people we started out as." I was bursting to ask what he had meant by that. He could see by my furrowed brow I was confused. "I don't expect you to understand that statement right now," he said "But I hope you will at the end of what we have to tell you, and you will no doubt have a few questions to ask, but I would ask of you to save them until the end of the story."

"I'll keep my lips sealed until the end," I said.

"Shall I go first?" asked Greg looking around the room at the others.

There was a unanimous agreement from everyone. He adjusted his cushion and settled back in his armchair. He took a deep breath and gave out an enormous sigh.

"It happened almost one year to the day." He paused for a moment and looked at each of them in turn. "I dare say there hasn't been a day we haven't thought about that incredible weekend." There were nods and grunts of agreement from the others. "Believe me, none of us are the sort given to wild exaggeration or fantasies, although after hearing this you may think otherwise. You may come to the conclusion it was a result of our brains being addled on drugs. You may be convinced it was a fantastic dream, but then how do you explain all four of us having the same dream at the same time? I assure you, Peter, it wasn't a dream, what the four of us experienced that weekend and the following few days was frighteningly real. You have to believe me when I say that every minute of our incredible experience is as clear as crystal. From that day on we have waited for someone to come along who we think will believe our unimaginable story and understand what we went through having to keep it to ourselves. Until we found that person, we all promised to remain tight lipped about it. Now if I am any judge of character, I believe we have found that person in you, Peter."

I was taken aback for a moment. I felt touched that these people, who apart from Greg, were complete strangers, were placing their full trust in me.

"Thank you, Greg," I answered "You can trust me to have an objective view. I know you will not be telling me what you term a fantastic story if it didn't have some substance."

Greg then related to me what was indeed an incredible story followed by each of the others in turn. If it had been told to me by any other person than Greg, I would have dismissed it as nonsense. Actually there are four different stories involved, but they all gel into one. What I mean by that is… Oh never mind. It's too complicated to explain. You will hear from the others later. I will let Greg take it from here.

5

"It was hot, unusually hot for the time of year, and very humid," began Greg. "I had not long been promoted to senior engineer at Blacks Engineering, and that was where I was to be found on the day before Good Friday, putting the finishing touches to a coal cutting machine ready to be shipped abroad. It was late in the afternoon and I was looking forward to the four days holiday ahead of me. I had just purchased yet another old Harley Davidson motorcycle, which I intended to strip and rebuild. Old motorcycles, particularly Harley Davidson's, were my hobby; I had three in various stages of refurbishment. Although I had planned to strip down my Harley, under normal circumstances I would have preferred for Sylvia and myself to get away for the four days like we always used to, but now, with Sylvia in a permanent alcoholic haze, there was little chance of that happening." Greg stopped his story and looked at me. "Sylvia was my wife, and you will see why she was like this later in the story." Greg continued. "She had broached the subject a couple of times as the weekend approached, but I dismissed the suggestion on the grounds she would never be able to stay sober that long and that the holiday would almost certainly descend into arguments. I had resigned myself to the fact that I was kidding myself if I thought she was going to improve now, and any conversation we had between us was a waste of breath because she wouldn't remember a word of it the next day. I have to admit I hadn't been the best husband to her, and whilst she had tried to hold our somewhat rocky marriage together, I thought only of my own needs, and so we just drifted along. I let the house and the garden deteriorate. I had no interest in anything only my motorcycles.

I glanced at my watch. It was just gone 4.30pm. Another hour or so and I would be packing away my tools and looking forward to the long weekend. Most of the workforce would have already been winding down, but I wanted to put the finishing touches to this machine before I finished for the holiday. I wanted to give myself a clear start after the Easter break, and all that would be needed when I returned would be to test out the machine ready for delivery.

Little did I know that Harry Baines, the works manager, was about to spoil my plans. I should have guessed as much when I saw him propelling his fat little body in my direction, but as soon as I saw his dozen or so strands of hair, which he normally kept plastered down across the front of his otherwise bald pate, dancing about like a demented puppet in the breeze, and the expression on his face, I knew it was trouble. He stood for a moment watching me test out the nut and bolt tensions. I carried on as though he wasn't there. I wasn't going to speak if he didn't, but I thought better of it. Knowing Harry, if I didn't say something he would have been there all night.

"What is it Harry?" I grunted.

"There's a bit of a panic on the Sandford Valley Mine."

"Panic," I echoed. "I suspect this panic is going to spoil my weekend, is it?"

"Well… err yes I know, I'm sorry about this," he spluttered, giving me his best hound dog expression. "But, only a day of it if we are lucky."

"What's the problem?" I growled. "It isn't even operating yet. What is so urgent it can't wait?"

"It seems they are bringing the official opening forward to Easter Monday, so they are insisting on a full inspection this weekend of all the equipment we have installed, because now they will be taking some VIPs underground as well as a tour of the complex."

"That's very nice of them," I said. "It doesn't matter about anyone else's weekend does it?"

"There's a bonus in it for you," Harry almost chirped. I didn't say or give any reaction to that; I just looked at him, waiting for him to tell me if there were other incentives. He knew what that look meant. "There will be double pay while you are there, plus an extra day off in lieu. I think that's very generous, Greg."

I would have been silly to refuse. In fact I was more than happy with the deal. Double pay would certainly come in handy, so would an extra day off. I wasn't going to tell Harry that though. "OK," I groaned. "I don't suppose I have much choice in the matter. I want Rod with me though."

"Yes, yes of course." He looked at his watch. "He should be home from that job at the quarry now; I'll give him a ring. I don't suppose he will be very happy about it either, but I could do with you getting over there first thing in the morning."

I told Harry not to worry, but to leave Rod to me. "I'll ring him," I said. "It will be better coming from me."

Harry looked at my scowling face. As works manager he was solely responsible for organising the workforce, but he could see I wasn't in the best of moods. He just nodded his head and handed me a note pointing to the name scribbled on it. "Bill Hodgkins the mine's safety officer will be there to take you down the mine. He will be doing his inspection at the same time." He scuttled off as fast as his fat little legs could carry him.

I muttered to myself all the way home. Normally I didn't mind working extra time. In fact the situation being as it was at home, I welcomed it. Sad to say it, but there was nothing for me to dash home for, except on this occasion I was looking forward to hiding myself in my workshop. I pulled into the drive and jumped from the car. I could hear music blaring away from the house. Sylvia was a big fan of the Rolling Stones, which was fine; I liked them too, although I must admit I was more of a Beatles fan. The problem was, that since the tragedy, she had played them non-stop and with increasing intensity. I rushed straight to the house. The blast of noise that hit my eardrums as I opened the door was horrendous. I hurried to the living room to find Sylvia prostrate on the sofa in a state of unconsciousness with a near empty bottle of whiskey on the side table and an empty glass clutched in her outstretched hand.

I switched off the record player and stood for a moment looking at her drawn features and sallow skin, asking myself what happened to that wonderful woman I had married? I had convinced myself I had tried everything possible and I was just beating my head against a brick wall. I was satisfied that I and the medical profession had done our best and there was no more we could do. I had made my mind up it was time to move on. I took the glass from her hand and placed it on the table and made my way into the hall to ring Rod and give him the bad news.

Rod was considered one of the best electrical engineers in the business, and it was he who had installed the complex wiring and electronics system for most of the machinery at the state-of-the-art new super pit. He didn't sound very pleased at the phone call.

"This sounds like trouble," he groaned before I had a chance to say anything.

"Now how do you know that?" I laughed.

"Because by now you would have been stuck into that Harley of yours. You've been talking of nothing else since you bought it, so it must be something important to keep you away from it."

"Yes you're right," I sighed. "There's a panic on at the Sandford Valley mine. Apparently they have brought the opening forward to Monday, so they now want the full inspection brought forward to tomorrow."

"Ok," he sighed. "I suppose if they insist on a full inspection then so be it. I can't see Dawn being very pleased though." I was quick to point out we were getting double pay and a day in lieu. "Well that's something I suppose," he said.

I was actually taken by surprise at the way Rod was taking the news. I expected him to put up more of a resistance but he seemed to be taking the interruption to his holiday in his stride. "I think the two of us should have any problems fixed fairly quickly," I said, trying to sound convincing. "But bring some lunch just in case."

"I'd like to take Jason with us," Rod suddenly blurted out.

At this point Greg stopped the story and looked at Jason. "I'm sorry son, but I have to relate all the facts as they were at the time."

Jason shrugged his shoulders. "That's ok Greg. That's the way it was."

"I have to confess," continued Greg. "I couldn't understand Rod's thinking. I questioned him on Jason's suitability. I knew he spent more time off sick than at the factory, and when he was there, his mind never seemed to be about his work. But Rod assured me he would take him in hand. "He'll make a good electrician if he puts his mind to it," he said. "This will be good training for him, and he'll come running when he knows there is a bit extra money in his pocket."

I was still doubtful about the wisdom of that decision, but Rod said he would accept responsibility for him. "Ok" I said. "But he had better not be late in the morning. I am not waiting for him."

"He'll be there," assured Rod. "Now I'd better go and break the news to Dawn. She isn't going to be very happy. We had planned to hitch the caravan up and drive down to the seaside."

"All being well we will be able to do the inspection in one day." I said confidently. "You will be able to tag the extra day onto your holiday so you will still be getting your four days; it's just that you will be starting a day later, that's all. Now I'd like to meet at the works at 8 o'clock tomorrow morning."

6

We all met up at the works at the agreed time, including Jason, which I must admit surprised me, and we set off for the Sandford Valley mine arriving there about 9 o'clock. Bill, the safety officer, was waiting for us at the lodge as arranged and took us along to the manager's office. The place was heaving with officials and delegates. I can't remember how many there were to be precise, but they were all milling about pretending to be the most important person there, giving their opinions on protocol and where to start the conducted tour and what route to take. Each of them interrupting each other with their point of view, you couldn't hear yourself think. You can imagine what a shambles they were going to make of the opening ceremony, but that was their problem. We completely ignored them and spread out the maps of the underground workings.

This new mine had two levels. The top level road had been cut heading west towards the old Hays Heath mine about three miles away as the crow flies and would eventually connect to their workings and serve as an escape route in case of emergency. The bottom level had been dug to reach a rich seam of coal which had been discovered just over a mile below the surface.

We decided we would start the inspection on the lower level. After an hour of route planning and a couple of cups of coffee, Bill took the three of us across to the lamp house for our lamps and helmets, then across to the cages for the descent. He then telephoned the winding house to advise him of our planned route and approximate time of return.

Rod and I had been down this mine several times, and Jason a couple of times when we were installing the machinery, so we knew what to expect, but even so, unless you are experienced at travelling in a pit cage, the sensation that your stomach has found its way into your mouth is a somewhat unpleasant experience.

With a ring of the warning bell the cage suddenly dropped like a stone, plummeting us into the bowels of the earth. This was an everyday occurrence to Bill who chatted merrily away until the cage suddenly slowed its rapid descent causing our knees to sag beneath us, until, with a jolt; it came to rest at the lower level. We piled out into the brightly lit, high roofed spacious area referred to as the pit bottom. Brand new tubs, neatly piled up with coal, were standing lined up like soldiers ready to be loaded into the cage, and were presumably on show for the dignitaries visit on Monday.

We passed by the small railway siding with open seated carriages which would transport the men to their respective places of work. Rod and I had travelled on this system many times before. This time though, as Bill wanted to check every inch of the roadways, we would be travelling by foot. So with Bill leading the way we set off.

After about a hundred yards the lighting disappeared and we switched on our helmet lamps. It was slow progress as Bill would stop and examine all the roof supports, making sure none of them had buckled or cracked. This is a routine inspection in any mine as there is regular movement of the ground. Jason would jump out of his skin every time he heard a groan or creak from the supports but it was quite a normal occurrence. It took us just over an hour to reach our first piece of equipment to test, then on to the coal cutting machine at the coal face. There had been a report of a malfunction on this particular machine. Rod isolated the power and I gave every part a good examination which revealed there was nothing wrong with it mechanically. It hadn't jammed so there was no reason why it hadn't been working. It pointed to an electrical problem so I handed over to Rod. Diving into his box and bringing out his testing equipment he threw the switch and tested all the circuits. After about twenty minutes he shook his head.

"It's working fine," he said. "If there was a problem it must have righted itself."

I made the suggestion that for some reason the switch may have tripped. Rod thought not, assuring me that everything was in perfect working order. He suggested we check out the rest of the machinery on this level and then do a check on the system on the top level in case the trouble stemmed from there. It was slow progress with Bill giving everything a thorough examination, but we finally checked out the last piece of equipment to our satisfaction before making our way back to the pit bottom.

We entered the cage and Bill gave the signal to haul us up to the top level. Here again shiny new tubs filled with coal were waiting for dignitaries inspection. We alighted from the cage and followed Bill on his inspection tour making our examination of the equipment as we went until we reached the main fan and the back-up fan located at the far end of the west roadway. These would be the final pieces of equipment to test.

"Only these to test now, Rod," I grinned. "I told you it would only take us a day. You can go on your caravan holiday tomorrow, and you can go and have a drink with your friends, Jason."

Rod then isolated the main fan, which should have been the signal for the other one to kick in, but it remained still. Isolating the power, Rod gave it a thorough examination. After about half an hour he finally shook his head and declared there was no reason why the back-up fan shouldn't be working.

Jason suggested it may be faulty motors, but Rod and I disputed that suggestion. I explained to Jason, you may get one faulty motor and if you were very unlucky you could get two, but there were six motors altogether in this system and it's very unlikely all six would go down at once. Rod then asked Bill if the Hays Heath fans were working.

"I assume they are," he answered. "I haven't heard any reports they are not. Why do you ask?"

"When I switched off the main fan I could still feel the air being pulled through. I thought it might have been pulled from Hays Heath."

Bill shook his head. "No, we haven't broken through yet, and in any case air doors would be fitted at the joining point; otherwise the two sets of fans would be working against each other."

Rod thought for a moment "Well I definitely felt a flow of air from somewhere. Let me switch it all off again." Rod again isolated the power bringing the fan to a stop. "There," he said. "Can you feel it?"

"You are right," exclaimed Bill. "There is definitely airflow from somewhere. Come on let's find out where it's coming from." With that he strode quickly off towards the end of the roadway with the rest of us following.

After about a hundred yards Bill came to an abrupt halt. He stood in complete silence staring ahead of him. "What on earth," he grunted. "Since when did they put that there?"

"What is it Bill?" I asked.

"He pointed ahead of him. Blasted air doors," he growled. "They never told me they had broken through to Hays Heath. They are not on my map. Somebody is going to get an earful when I get back." He made towards the doors. "No wonder you can feel an air flow, the darn things are open. Heads are going to roll over this I can tell you." Bill squeezed himself through the air doors and we followed. He stood shining his lamp up the roadway. "This is Hays Heath we are in now," he announced. "I worked for many years at this mine, I recognise these workings. They haven't worked this seam for years. There is a bit of coal left but it was too unproductive to mine. In fact I don't think they work any of these seams anymore. Most of the coal is now being dug from the other side."

I pointed out to Bill, that now we were on this side I couldn't feel any air circulating like before. He stood stock still for a moment before wetting his finger and holding it in the air. I could see in the lamplight he had a deep frown on his face.

"That's strange," he said. "The fans must be on the blink here as well, but there has been no report of that. I would have heard about it."

"Thought you said they didn't work this part of the mine anymore?" I asked.

"They don't," he replied. "They stopped working this part about two years ago."

"Then surely they wouldn't need to run the fans anymore would they?"

"Normally they wouldn't, but with plans for the two mines to join up, they have to keep the fans running to keep the air clear. Obviously they have already broken through, so why the fans are not running is a mystery, unless some idiot has closed the air doors further on." He then pointed down the roadway informing us that the ventilation shaft in this area was about half a mile away.

Jason complained he was on the point of starvation and suggested we stop for a bite to eat. Bill was adamant we carry on to see what the problem was, saying it would be too risky in these old workings to remain without air circulating. We followed him along the roadway until we came to another set of air doors. Bill stopped in his tracks.

"I can't remember any air doors being fitted here either," he exclaimed. "At least not while I was working at this mine. They must have been fitted recently for some reason."

We all passed through the doors and followed Bill along the black airless tunnel. All the while Bill was muttering about not remembering this part of the mine. At last we reached the fans. They were silent. Jason tested the electrics and announced that there was nothing wrong and there was no reason why they were not working.

"We had better get back and report it," said Bill. Jason again complained that he was hungry and thirsty. Bill gave a big sigh and conceded that perhaps we should stop for a moment. "Not too long though," were his words as we all found a comfortable spot to rest our weary legs. He then advised three of us to switch off our lamps to save the batteries.

We must have been more tired than we thought. It felt like we had trudged these dark tunnels for hours on end, and now with some food and a hot drink inside us we all relaxed and closed our eyes for about ten minutes or so, it didn't feel like any longer than that. The next thing I knew was Bill jumping to his feet and suggesting we make our way to the back to the Sandford Valley mine.

It seemed to take twice as long to retrace our steps back. All the while Bill was looking about him and muttering. I asked him if there was a problem. His answer sent a shudder down my spine.

"If I were to be honest," he replied. "I don't know where I am. I thought I knew these workings like the back of my hand, but I don't recognise these roadways at all."

"Are you telling us we are lost," cried Jason, a little panic showing in his voice.

"No of course not," assured Bill. "All I am saying is, I don't recognise these workings but if we go back exactly the way we came we can't go wrong."

We all agreed it would be the sensible thing to do and wasted no time in moving forward, sticking very close to Bill. We reached the last air door and we all filtered through one by one, making our way along the workings until we reached the end of the roadway. The air door which had connected the old mine to the new one, the very one which we had passed through earlier, was no longer there, it was just a blank wall.

"What the heck is going on here?" barked Bill. "We can't have gone wrong, it's a straight roadway."

"You have to be wrong, Bill," I said. "We came through a set of air doors, and there is none here. We must have taken a wrong turning."

"I tell you this is the right place," he insisted. "This is how it was left when the seam ran out, I recognise the workings." He pointed to a solid wall. "The air doors we came through were definitely there."

"Well, they are not here now," cried Jason. "They can't just have disappeared, can they?"

But Bill was having none of it. He was adamant he had followed the correct route back. "You can't go wrong," he had insisted. "Back through those air doors at Hays heath and follow the road. That's the way we went and that is the way we came back."

I couldn't disagree with him. He had to be right, but where were those air doors? Jason started to panic, shouting we were lost and we would never find our way out. Rod calmed him down by saying that the roads must lead to somewhere, all we had to do was to follow them and they would eventually end up somewhere Bill would recognise.

I remember Bill lifting his hard hat and scratching at his head. "I don't understand it," he said. "We followed a straight road to the air doors, and all we have done is re-trace our steps back to the same spot. Those air doors should be here."

Jason was panicking more by the minute though. "But they are not here," he snapped.

Rod calmed him down for the second time. "Panicking isn't going to do any good, Jason," he said. "Bill will get us out of here, don't worry about that."

Bill pointed back up the roadway from the direction we had come. "The only practical thing is to go back to where we started from and look again," he suggested.

Once again we backtracked to the Hays Heath air doors. Nobody spoke all the way back. I wasn't panicking like Jason but I was very apprehensive. I couldn't help thinking about those doors. Bill was right about them, they should have been there, and he was right about the way back, and if the truth were known we all knew he was right. What none of us could come to terms with, was what had happened to those doors.

We arrived back at the air doors and made our way through them. We waited for   directions from Bill. He stood for a moment shining his light about. "This was the old main roadway without doubt," he said. "Why those air doors were built is a mystery. There is no reason for them." He then pointed ahead of him. "This way," he beckoned.

We must have trudged along that road for a good hour with Jason muttering all the way. I don't know about the others but I was praying with all my might that Bill was leading us in the right direction. He came to a sudden halt and pointed to a set of doors to our right. "Through there," he urged. "These should bring us to the main workings."

We filed through into another narrow roadway. "This is a short cut from the main workings to the old workings," he assured us. I felt better now that Bill seemed to have his bearings. After about fifty yards we reached another set of doors which we went through. Bill was the last through and stood for a moment shining his light about him. I noted a slight frown on his face. "

What is it, Bill?" I asked.

He pointed to three coal tubs lashed to a thick wire cable stretching into the distance with groups of three tubs lashed to the cable at intervals. "There's nothing moving," he said. "That cable should be moving all the time, as you can see its deathly quiet."

"Well, it's Easter isn't it?" said Jason. "Nobody will be working."

Bill shook his head. "Apart from the main holidays, a coal mine never stops. There is always coal being drawn."

I suggested we get to the pit bottom and find out what the problem is when we get there. I admit I was uneasy with the deafening silence about the place. There was nothing moving, not a sound of machinery on the go and not a human being in sight.

Eventually we reached the pit bottom. Immediately we all felt a little less claustrophobic in the spacious, brightly lit high roofed area, but I guessed they were all feeling the same as I did, and would feel much better stepping out of that cage and into the world above us. It was an eerie atmosphere as the four of us stood in total silence looking about us, hoping, I suppose, that the place would suddenly spring to life. There were a dozen or so coal laden tubs patiently waiting for someone, anyone, to push them into the eagerly awaiting cage.

"What now, Bill?" I asked.

"Everybody in the cage," he said. "Let's hope the winding man is at his station."

Nobody said a word as we all piled into the cage. Bill pulled the safety gates across, took a deep breath, then gave the signal on the bell to take us up. We all held our breath but the cage remained still. I don't know about Jason, but I was now the one beginning to panic. Bill gave the signal again. It seemed an eternity before the cage gave a little jerk, then remained still again, then with a jolt it began to rise slowly before gathering pace.

"Thank God for that" screamed Jason. "Don't ever ask me to go down a mine again."

I know how he felt. It was all I could do to stop myself getting to my knees and praying, and I swear I could see tears of joy down Rod's face. The cage slowed and eased itself to a halt. The world had never looked so good, albeit I was looking at it through the huge double doors of the warehouse-like building we had come to rest in. I was too busy looking about the place to take in the fact, until Bill pointed it out, that there was no one there to let us out of the cage. In fact there didn't seem to be anyone about at all. It was almost as quiet as it was below ground. Bill opened the cage security grill. At the same time the outer one slid open as if worked by a pair of unseen hands. Bill stepped from the cage with the rest of us following as quickly as we could in case it decided to descend again. We made our way outside into what I can only describe as like a scene from one of those ghost towns you see in the old cowboy films. You know the ones, where the rickety old wooden buildings are standing silent, and little swirls of dust and sagebrush are blowing along the deserted main street. As far as we could see the whole pit complex seemed to be lifeless. Nothing was moving, nobody was about, and not a sign of life could be seen or heard. Normally a colliery is a noisy place with the air full of whistles and warning hooters and steam operated machinery releasing their excess of steam and the constant noise of fully laden coal tubs rattling their way to the wharf to be unloaded would be heard. But it was eerily silent; you could almost hear a pin drop.

Bill was unable to get his head around what was happening and decided he was going up to see the engine man who was controlling the cage operation. None of us knew what to do next so we followed him to the winding house. We ascended a flight of stairs to the control room. Bill rapped on the door and waited. No one was allowed to enter the winding house until you were given permission, as the notice on the door emblazoned in large red letters informed you. Bill banged on the door again, still there was no answer. He asked me to look to see if the cage wheels were moving. I shook my head when I saw they were at rest. He banged on the door again, but this time, when there was no answer, he flung the door open and strode inside. I can't forget that look on his face as he stood open mouthed at the door for a moment. As none of us, other than Bill, were familiar with the rules and regulations regarding the running of a coal mine, we didn't fully understand what went on in a winding house other than it was where the cages were operated from.

"I don't believe this," snarled Bill. "These places are manned day and night. There should be at least four people in here at any one time. He shook his head in disbelief. "I don't know what on earth is going on," he said as he surveyed the room with a perplexed look on his face. The engines were silent as was the rest of the engine room. The thick steel hawsers which wound themselves around the massive drums were perfectly still, and on examination, Bill found the controls were locked. I could see the blood draining from his face. It was plain to see he was in a state of shock. "The machinery is cold," he said. "This means it hasn't been working for quite a while."

"But it's just pulled us up," voiced Rod. "Someone must have done that."

"It doesn't make sense," grunted Bill. "I don't understand any of this."

Jason was all for getting out of the place quickly, bemoaning the fact that the place was giving him the creeps." We all agreed with that statement and made our way outside. Bill suggested we go and deposit our lamps and hard hat in the lamp room, and then do a tour of the area to see if there was anyone about, and try and figure out what was going on.

As we marched over to the lamp house, Jason pointed out how odd the sky looked. Everywhere was bathed in a light pastel yellow haze from horizon to horizon as though it had been given a colour wash. There was no visible Sun, although it was fairly light. Even though it was unusual, it wasn't on our priority list right then. The main concern was where had everybody disappeared to?

The scene at the lamp house was a repeat of that at the winding house. Not a soul was to be seen. We took off our hard hats and hung up our lamps then set off to tour the complex. For over an hour we toured the site, visiting everywhere where we would have expected someone to have been working, starting with the Manager's office. We even inspected the baths and the canteen; anywhere where there would likely be someone to tell us what on earth was happening. The strangest part was, although the place had the appearance of working normally, it was utterly bereft of life. Not even the car park had a single car on it. The whole scenario was bizarre, and gave me the strangest feeling in the pit of my stomach. There had hardly been a word spoken during our tour of the pit complex. I suppose mainly because all questions had been asked and to which none had an answer, plus events had overtaken us and had numbed our senses.

Bill eventually led us back to the manager's office where he had the idea of ringing the Sandford Valley mine to report our findings. He tried several times to ring out, but the phone lines were dead. Finally he gave up and suggested we make our way back to Sandford Valley to let them know about the peculiar situation here.

"How are we going to get there?" asked Jason.

"We'll have to walk," replied Bill.

Jason wasn't happy with that. "Walk?" he growled. "It's five miles by road. I can't walk five miles."

"Perhaps we won't have to," I said. "If we walk to the main road, we may be able to get a lift."

"No we won't," he replied tetchily. "There's nobody about is there? Everybody has vanished into thin air. There's nobody out there to give us a lift."

I couldn't help but raise my voice at this point. Jason had such a negative attitude at times. "And how do you know that?" I barked. "The whole world won't have vanished will it?" He never gave me an answer. He just stared at me and shrugged his shoulders. To be honest I could understand him being angry and frustrated. I think we were all feeling a little frustrated and scared at this point having gone through a very strange and frightening experience. None of us would ever have admitted it, but there wasn't one of us who, when we were trekking through those dark tunnels a couple of hours ago, thought we were ever going to see light of day again, and when we finally reached the surface thinking that our ordeal was now over, we were then faced with even more frustration of the extraordinary sight of a deserted mine complex. All we wanted to do was to get home and forget what had happened, but little did we know, our perplexing experiences had only just begun.

"Let us just calm down, shall we?" intervened Rod. "We are not going to get anywhere shouting at each other."

"Just a minute," said Bill. "I noticed a mini bus outside the bathhouse. There's a chance the keys may be still in it."

We made for the bus with fingers crossed. We were in luck, the keys were in the   ignition and the fuel tank gauge was reading full. We piled inside and threw our exhausted bodies on the seats. We were soon on our way with Bill in the driving seat.

As we made our journey to the Sandford Valley mine, it seemed Jason may well have been right in his little outburst. The whole scene was deserted. As I scanned the rolling fields there were no signs of life. This was a farming county, but there were no animals grazing in the fields as you would expect there to be. No farmers on their tractors going about their business, no birds flying about. There was a "Told you so," from Jason having a little dig at me. I answered him by saying that it was now early Easter Sunday morning and most people would either be having a lie in or were away on holiday. I just got a blank stare from him. Whether he actually believed it or not, I couldn't tell. I couldn't blame him if he hadn't. I didn't even convince myself that this was the case.

7

We had just entered the small village of Weston Sandford, and it came as no surprise to any of us to find that this pretty little village also appeared to be deserted. I told myself it was only a small village of about two hundred residents or so, and it *was* early Sunday morning, but then I argued with myself, you would expect someone to be up and about. Unlike us city folk, most country people tended to be early risers, Sundays no exception. I at least expected to see someone taking the dog for a walk or a horse trotting along the road being exercised, and where was the obligatory farmer? who at any other time would have been blocking the road with his tractor or a herd of cows. Right now they would have been warmly welcome. There was nothing though, just empty roads and empty fields. I was beginning to feel twinges of alarm growing. This just couldn't be real. Then something happened to which none of us had an answer.

Nobody commented as Bill drove very slowly through the village. If they were anything like me there was too much going on in their heads to say anything; I suppose we were all straining our eyes looking for any sign of life. Two miles on through the village, we reached the turn off for the Sandford Valley mine. We rounded the corner when Bill brought the vehicle to a shuddering halt.

"What is it, Bill?" I asked.

"There's something wrong here," he said staring ahead of him. "This road was made into a dual carriage way some years ago."

"You must have taken a wrong turning," commented Jason.

"No I haven't," snapped Bill. "You can't go wrong. There is only one road in and out of the mine." He pointed across the field to a white painted stone house. That's Briggs farm across there. Harry Brigg owned all this land; he made a fortune when he sold it off to the mine company. I've travelled this road many times when they were just starting to build the place."

"You are right, Bill," said Rod. "This was a dual carriageway when Greg and I used to come here to install the equipment. Isn't that right, Greg?"

I studied the landscape and had to agree with him. It was definitely this road, but what we were looking at was no more than a country lane as it used to be. My brain was beginning to struggle to find a logical solution.

Bill slammed the bus into gear and set off again. We had only gone about a mile along the road when he again brought the bus to a skidding halt. I asked him what the problem was this time. He just pointed to a huge sign which read. Site of the proposed SANDFORD VALLEY SUPERPIT.

"What's the problem?" asked Rod.

Bill again pointed at the sign. "Look at what it says. Start date April 1972."

"It's just an old sign," I said.

"No," grunted Bill. "They pulled that sign down a long time ago when the road was widened to take all the construction traffic." He shook his head in frustration. "There is something funny going on here and I don't like it."

I had to agree with him on that point. For the short time I had known him, Bill had always given me the impression he was not the sort of person given to panic. During the strange goings on below ground, he had always kept his cool, and I had no doubt his level headed approach to the situation we were in, and his coolness had kept me from panicking. I'm pretty sure that went for the other lads too, but unsurprisingly these strange events were beginning to unnerve all of us.

We proceeded again for another half mile. By now we should have been at the mine entrance, but as we rounded a bend we had an uninterrupted view across the valley. We sat dumbfounded as we viewed the area where the mine was supposed to be. We were staring at empty green meadows.

"This is impossible," ranted Bill. He pointed across the valley. "Look there's Jacob's wood. It was the first area to be cleared when they moved those huge machines in. It was a bad day when they tore those trees down. It was a beautiful little wood, I spent many happy hours playing in there as a lad. In the spring a carpet of bluebells would cover the entire ground. It was a very popular spot with the locals, and there was a massive protest there when it was heard it was going to be cut down. People were chaining themselves to the trees and lying in front of the bulldozers, but it didn't make any difference, they still tore the wood apart, and look, there's Hartlet's farm which was bulldozed as well. What on earth is going on?"

"It's like we've gone back in time." Commented Rod.

I think he was just talking to himself, but Jason snapped at him. "Back in time?" He growled. "What are you talking about, back in time?"

Poor old Rod was taken aback, saying it was a loose comment and he was just mooting an explanation for it. But Jason wasn't to be pacified, accusing Rod of being stupid and had been reading too many science fiction books. To his credit, Rod just sighed and said nothing. It was obvious Jason wasn't coping too well with the situation, and although we all found the circumstances frustrating, none of us had an explanation, and none of us knew what to do, but there was only one thing we could do now and that was to head for Garton. What we would find there was any one's guess.

We headed back up the lane to the junction where we turned and headed for home. It was total silence all the way as we all stared out of the window onto an empty world. It was like looking at a huge photograph. There was nothing moving. The fields were empty of all life. Not a horse or cow or sheep or any kind of animal could be seen. There was not even a sighting of a single bird making its way across that monotonous yellow sky. It was the weirdest, most frightening of experiences.

We entered the outskirts of Garton. The picture here, not unexpectedly, was a repeat of what we had seen on our journey, only this time, seeing a place as large as Garton completely deserted, brought home to us the reality of the situation. Bill pulled the bus to a halt and stared down the empty main street, utter disbelief etched across his face. For a few moments we all just sat and stared out of the window at the unnerving sight around us.

"I must be having a nightmare," uttered Rod. "Wake me up somebody. For God's sake wake me up." The exasperation inside of him was plain to see.

A feeling of helplessness had now overwhelmed me, and I had no doubt the others felt this way too. Questions were racing through my mind. Where was everybody? What had happened to them? Why was it happening? I jumped up from my seat and made my way off the bus. Bill called after me asking me where I was going. I couldn't answer him because I didn't know what to do or where I was going, but my confused and tormented brain was telling me I had to do something. I started to walk the empty pavement of the main street. Bill jumped from the bus and raced to catch me. There was no conversation between us as we walked side by side along the road, but I knew we both had our eyes and ears alert to catch any sign of life. Oh how I longed to hear a barking dog or see a cat rummaging in a dustbin to relieve the unbearable feeling we were completely alone on this planet. There was nothing though, not a creak of a door or a tin can rolling about, or even the rustle of a paper bag blowing down the street. In fact there was no breeze at all, not even the faintest movement of air, just that awful deafening silence.

After an hour of parading the streets and getting no nearer to finding out the cause of this phenomenon, we decided to head back to the vehicle where

Rod and Jason were waiting. Bill climbed into the driver's seat and we all sat in silence. After a couple of minutes, he turned and looked at us.

"I think we are all putting off doing this," he said. "But I think we ought to go to our respective homes and see what has happened to our families, but I think we will only be confirming the inevitable, so please be prepared."

Off we set through the desolate town. Not only had the inhabitants vanished but so had every form of transport. The only vehicle was the one we were in. I believe we were all thinking it must be an elaborate dream, or more like a nightmare as far as I was concerned, but what was convincing me it wasn't a dream, was the fact that when you are dreaming, you don't know you are dreaming. You don't ask yourself if you are dreaming as I was doing now, do you?

The first stop was Rod's house. As we pulled to halt, he slid back the door, and without saying a word he leapt from the bus like a shot from a gun and ran as fast as he could down the drive and disappeared into the house. We waited quite a while for him, when finally he came staggering out of the house as though he was drunk. He could hardly make it up the drive and was visibly suffering great torment. I thought he was going to keel over there and then so I jumped out and ran to him to give him support. He collapsed onto the drive saying he wanted to remain there and look for Dawn. He understandably wasn't thinking straight. I suggested to him, as we didn't know what was happening or why, it was best we all stuck together. If we all parted company who knows what might happen, we may never see each other again. Fortunately he saw the sense in this and agreed to return to the bus. He sank exhausted into his seat, and taking a couple of minutes to recover he turned to me and started to apologise. I of course assured him there was no need as we were all experiencing the same helpless feeling.

"All I could think of at the time," interrupted Rod "Was that I wanted to be with Dawn. I know I had seen with my own eyes that everyone had simply vanished, but the thought that she wouldn't be at home never entered my head. I searched the house twice from top to bottom. I even looked under the beds and in cupboards in case she was playing tricks and hiding from me. That was the state of my utterly confused mind. When I couldn't find her, the reality of it all hit me like a ton of bricks. I couldn't think straight, I didn't know what to do to get my Dawn back. That is when I staggered outside in a flood of tears and sank to my knees, my mind a complete blank. I could just make out Greg running towards me and helping me to my feet and trying to get me back in the bus, but all I wanted to do was to stay and search the neighbourhood in case she was wandering the streets. I don't know why I thought that, there was no logic in the thinking, but then again there was no logic to any of it."

"I told Rod that there was no sense to any of what was going on," continued Greg. "I'm sure there will be a simple explanation," I told them. "But until we can fathom what it is, we have all got to stick together."

Bill's was the next nearest house, and that is where we headed. As we sped through the deserted streets taking in the desolate scene, it was becoming increasingly likely we were completely alone in this town, and not unlikely, we were alone in the country, and the frightening thought had crossed my mind that we may also be alone in the world.

We eventually reached the street where Bill lived. For some reason he was in no hurry to get home. He drove at a leisurely pace along the deserted thoroughfare, scanning every house intently on the way before sliding gently to a halt outside his house.

He switched off the engine and just sat there staring at the house. "We have lived here for over 30 years," he said "And it's never looked as good as it does today." He continued staring at it for a few moments, his eyes searching the windows for signs of life. Goodness knows what was going through his mind. "Funny though," he said after a brief silence. "I am in no hurry to go into the house. Of course I am just delaying the inevitable, because I know, as everybody knows, there will be nobody there." Then he lapsed into silence again. I sat there just looking at him. I didn't know what to say. "I don't want to do this," he said abruptly.

"I think you ought to go in," was the only thing I could think to say to him.

"Why?" he asked sullenly. "It's pointless. I am just going into an empty house."

I knew this was what Bill was afraid of more than anything. He had witnessed the empty world passing before his eyes and the deserted houses of that village we had passed through, and up until now he had taken everything on the chin, but the one thing he dreaded was the thought of walking into his own house to find it totally void of life, which would finally bring the reality of the situation home to him. I had used all my powers of persuasion to eventually get him to check out the house; labouring the point that if he did not, he would always regret not making sure. "What if there is someone in there waiting and wondering what has happened to you?" I asked.

After much thought, Bill slowly eased back the sliding door and made his way to the house. He was gone for about fifteen minutes, not long in the scheme of things, but it seems a long time when you are waiting for someone. He re-appeared from the house and began walking slowly towards the bus, his face pale and drawn, and jumped back in the driver's seat. I asked if he was ok, to which he nodded and gave a feeble yes. It was no good asking questions; we all knew what the answers would be.

"There's no one there of course," he suddenly blurted out, before lapsing into a brief silence. "Something strange happened at the house," he then said very matter-of-factly. We all looked at him waiting to hear what it was. "I could see the door was closed as I walked down the drive as I expected it to be," he continued. "I was just taking the key from my pocket as I approached. I was just about to insert the key when the door slowly swung open. I was sure I had locked it before going to work. It was one of those ritualistic things I did automatically. The other strange thing was, it didn't make that awful squeak which always emanated from the hinges every time the door opened and closed. I had promised myself every time I heard it I would silence it, but I never did get around to it. I put it to the back of my mind momentarily and entered the house, shouting as I did so, asking if anyone was there, but it was deathly quiet. I searched every room in the house, everywhere I could think of, but it only confirmed what I already knew. At least it satisfied my mind that the place was empty, as you said it would be, Greg."

Nobody, including me, made any comment. It was no use trying to offer an explanation for these strange events. We hadn't managed to come up with any answers so far, so it was no use trying to figure out an explanation for Bill's odd experience. He then turned to Jason. "You next," he said.

"No point!" replied Jason bluntly, staring through the window, his face as black as thunder. I asked him what he was talking about. "Will anybody be there?" he growled. "No there won't," he snarled answering his own question. "The place was empty when I left, and it will be empty when I get back. It's a waste of time going in." I looked at the others. They just shrugged their shoulders. Rod mouthed 'leave him be.' I said no more to him and turned to Bill. "Take me to my house then Bill."

It took us about thirty minutes from where we were to reach the house. Bill slowly eased the vehicle along the unmade dirt road, coming to a halt by the gate. I remember Rod commenting I was shaking like a leaf. To be honest, I was scared to death of going in the house. I realised now it was happening to me, how the others had felt when they went to inspect their houses.

I just sat there, I wanted to go in but I didn't want to find it empty and Sylvia gone. Despite what had gone on between us, and the apparent hopelessness of Sylvia's situation, I didn't want any harm to come to her. I knew in my heart, that she would not be there. Why would I be the only one whose loved ones had not disappeared? Finally I plucked up the courage to open the door and enter the house - my worst fears were confirmed. Like Jason and Bill, I combed the house from top to bottom hoping everything would be different in my house, but found the place empty. My mind was in torment as I realised I was in this horrible world where my loved ones and friends had all vanished for no apparent reason. I even tried the telephone but the line was dead. My head was swimming, my brain was in turmoil at the final realisation it was all real and not a nightmare I was experiencing. The last thing I remember is collapsing on the sofa; this very sofa as it happens, and blacking out.

Bill told me afterwards that the others had waited as long as they could. They were worried because I was so long, and decided to come and see if I was ok, and this is where they found me apparently, fast asleep. As the day's events had taken their toll on everyone and they were all in a near state of collapse, their brains simply unable to take any more, they left me where I was and made for the beds upstairs and fell asleep.

8

I was the first to wake the next morning to that strange yellow glow filling the room. I hadn't a clue what time it was or how long I had been asleep, I don't think I cared at that particular moment, but there was no doubt I was feeling more refreshed after my sleep. Now perhaps I would be able to think more clearly.

I made my way into the kitchen to make a cup of coffee. As I stood staring through the window waiting for the water to boil, reflecting what had gone on and trying to figure out what could have happened to everybody, I suddenly thought about my beloved motorcycles. I grabbed my keys from the hook and rushed to open the workshop doors. I looked in disbelief as only three out of my collection of eight were there.

Forgetting the trauma of what we had been through, I ranted and cursed about thieves and wanting their hands cutting off, when I suddenly remembered Rod had mentioned the fact that it looked like we may have gone back in time. This seemed to prove his theory, as I did only have three Harleys to start with. I had only added to my collection this last couple of years. I heaved a sigh of relief and closed and locked the doors and strolled back into the kitchen to make that coffee.

As I stood staring blankly out of the kitchen window gently sipping on my coffee and trying to think what steps we were going to take next, I had the strangest feeling I was being watched. I turned around expecting one of the lads to be there, but there was no one. I sat myself down at the kitchen table and continued with my thoughts. Again I had that feeling that eyes were upon me. My first thought was that one of the boys was playing a trick on me, so I made my way to the living room expecting one of them to be hiding in there. I should have known they wouldn't be in the mood to be fooling about like that in the situation we were in, but then again nothing made sense so far. I entered the room and stood dumbfounded as I could see the television was on. There was no sound, it just showed a peculiar looking man, if it was a man, staring at me from the screen. I couldn't figure out if it was male or female, or indeed if it was human. At this point I couldn't have cared less and assumed it was some rubbish sci-fi film being shown. I was about to switch it off when it dawned on me, that if the television was on, then there must be someone out there to broadcast it. My heart skipped a beat. There must be life out there somewhere I told myself. I ran from the room, shouting as I bounded up the stairs. "The television. The television."

Bill was just getting dressed. "What the heck is going on?" he asked.

"The television," I cried excitedly.

"What about the television?" Asked Rod, who was now wide awake and sitting on the edge of the bed.

"Come see, it's on." I leapt down the stairs two at a time with others following. We piled into the living room, but to my horror the screen was blank. I fiddled with the dials in desperation but there was nothing.

"You must have dreamt it, Greg," said Rod.

"No I didn't dream it!" I snapped back. "I was in the kitchen having a coffee. I wandered in here and this was on showing a funny creature."

"I'm sorry, Greg," insisted Rod. "You must have dreamt it, look at this." He pointed to the power cable. "It's not plugged in. It hasn't even got a plug on it."

I was dumbstruck. I felt so foolish as I was certain I had seen a face on the screen. But the proof was there, I couldn't have. I felt deflated, and as if trying to cope with all the other strange goings on wasn't enough, I was now having delusions. I'll give Bill and Rod credit–they made no adverse comments. They just said stranger things have happened and probably a lot more of that kind of thing will happen before we get to the bottom of it all. Jason of course gave a wry smile as much as to say he thought I was cracking up, but who could blame him? I thought I was too.

I offered to make everyone a coffee and breakfast. We all piled into the kitchen and sat around the table, discussing what we were going to do next. Jason who had complained earlier that he'd suffered a bad night, was now falling asleep at the table. Rod suggested he lay on the sofa for a few minutes until breakfast was ready.

We had been casually passing ideas back and forth for about fifteen minutes trying to figure out our next move. I was rummaging in the cupboards to find something for breakfast when I could hear another voice from the living room. I put my fingers to my lips to stop the others talking and listened.

"Sounds as though he's talking in his sleep," said Bill. I wasn't convinced though. It didn't sound like Jason's voice. I made for the living room with the others following. To my astonishment Jason was still fast asleep but the television was back on. I looked at Jason to see if he was pretending to be asleep but he was well away. I thought he had awoken and put it on to try and find some news and had fallen back to sleep. After shouting and shaking him for a couple of minutes, I finally aroused him. I asked him if he had put the TV on, when I remembered there wasn't a plug on it.

"Look at that," said Bill pointing to a strange figure on the screen. I know this sounds very odd, but it didn't seem to be part of the screen. It was like a 3D image, if you know what I mean. I still couldn't make out if it was male or female. Its skin was extremely pale, almost translucent. It had huge, and I mean huge, pale yellow almond shaped eyes. I could only see the head and shoulders, but it appeared to be painfully thin and was wrapped in a luminous blue cape. Whatever it was had stopped talking the moment we entered the room and was now sitting perfectly still and seemed to be staring at us. He, she, it, suddenly vanished from the screen.

"There," I said. "I told you I had seen something. What do you make of that?"

Bill and Rod just stared at each other. Bill commented about it being some sci-fi film, but then I pointed out that the television was unplugged. It was another weird happening to which none of us, yet again, had an explanation. We were now getting so used to them we put it to the back of our minds.

Bill asked me if I had a plan of action. I couldn't think of anything but to scout around the town and try to find some clues as to what had happened. As we were discussing our next move, Jason and Rod entered the room. Rod pointed to the television.

"I wonder who that is," he growled. "Why does he keep appearing like this?"

We couldn't believe it, especially when I pointed out again that the television was unplugged. We stared at the screen. It was that creature again. This time he was standing side on and pointing to something in the background. Then as suddenly as it appeared, the screen went blank. We all looked at each other for a moment. There was no explanation for this peculiar phenomenon, and certainly no meaning to it, so we turned our attention to our next move. I suggested to Rod and Jason, as I had done to Bill, that we scout the town to see if there would be any clues as to what had happened. Rod shrugged his shoulders saying, as there wasn't an alternative plan it was at least worth a try, so we bundled into the minibus and headed for the centre of town.

We drove slowly along the main street in complete silence. It was a spooky, unbelievable sight. We all felt as though we were in a terrible dream as we stared at the deserted streets. There was no one to be seen. There was not even a cat or a dog wandering about, and the strangest of all there was no traffic. No cars or trucks or buses, even the car parks were empty. I don't mind admitting, I was frightened by the whole scenario.

Bill halted the mini bus at the side of the road. "I think we should take a look inside some of the buildings," he suggested.

"What for?" growled Jason. "There's no one here, is there?"

Bill glared at him. "Because there just maybe someone in one of those buildings. There may be people just like us wondering what on earth has happened."

It was obvious it was now becoming a bit too much for Jason to handle. He looked to me to be on the verge of panic. I had to try and take his mind off it for a while. I pointed across the street. "There's a hotel across there, Jason. If you don't feel like walking about, you might be able to help yourself to a drink in there."

His face paled. "You are not leaving me alone. Who knows what might happen. Can't we all go for a drink?"

"Maybe just one, later," interrupted Rod. "I want a look around first though. We are not going to find anything sitting around drinking, are we?"

We all piled out of the bus and looked about us. I think each one of us was hoping to be the first to catch sight of anything moving. "In a situation like this," I said. "I would normally suggest we split up, but as things are, I think it wiser we all stick together." There was a chorus of agreement, especially from Jason who was so close to Rod he might as well have been tied to him.

Bill pointed towards the precinct. "Might as well start there," he said already heading towards it with the rest of us following. We maintained a leisurely pace along the wide pedestrian tree lined avenue, our eyes darting from one spot to another for signs of life or any clues of their existence.

Bill came to a sudden halt and pointed ahead of him towards a deserted bus station. "That bus station was knocked down years ago to build a new shopping centre. What's happening here?" He looked at me for an answer. I didn't have one of course.

"This proves my theory," exclaimed Rod. "We have managed to travel back in time. I was convinced he was right, but Bill and Jason stared at him with looks which said he was losing the plot. "I know it sounds incredible," he said. "But look at the evidence. The air doors which had disappeared in Sandford Valley when we went back to them. The mine itself had not even been built when we arrived at the site, and now this, a bus station in front of you which was knocked down some years ago. Has anyone else got any other explanation?" He was greeted with silence from Bill and the usual shrug of the shoulders from Jason.

"I agree with you, Rod," I said. "It is the only possible explanation."

Then I remember Jason making us all jump out of our skins. "Look," he yelled, pointing to a television set in a shop window, "Look at this."

We all stopped and looked. To my amazement it was that weird creature again in the same pose as before, pointing at something in the background. I hurried as fast as I could to the shop window. I wanted to see what he was pointing at before the screen went blank. I stared hard at it. Was it trying to tell us something? I concentrated my gaze on what the figure was indicating to. "If I'm not mistaken," I said. "That's Battersea Power Station he's pointing to in the background." They all gathered around. There was a chorus of agreement, but Jason was of course his usual negative self.

"What about it?" he grunted. "So it's Battersea Power Station. What has that got to do with anything?" I was rapidly losing patience with Jason's negativity and told him so in no uncertain terms. Maybe I was clutching at straws and maybe it meant nothing, but maybe it did, but I had to consider the facts. We appeared to have travelled back in time to a lifeless world where there are no other human beings, in fact no other creatures at all. We hadn't the faintest idea how we had ended up there, or why, and what is more we hadn't got a clue what to do next. Now someone, or something, which kept appearing on a television set, which wasn't even switched on, had appeared again, repeatedly pointing to Battersea Power Station. It had to have some significance as far as I was concerned. As I have said, maybe I was clutching at straws, but what else had we to go on?

I suggested we make our way to London and on to Battersea Power Station. I looked at each of them in turn as they stood in silence. I could almost see what they were thinking. Probably thought I was losing it to want to travel all that way because some weirdo on the television was pointing at it. Rod stated that the power station was now closed down and couldn't see why, of all the places in London, there would be anyone there. I had to agree with his reasoning, but we had to try something. "What have we got to lose? I asked. "What other plans do we have? There is obviously no one here. At least let us go and see if there is anyone else out there."

I looked at Jason who had remained silent. He looked away from my gaze and gave a matter of fact shrug of the shoulders, which was his trademark way of saying it was ok by him, but he would not be part of the blame if anything went wrong.

We returned to the house, where I suggested we load up the bus with food and blankets and anything else we may need on the journey and then get a good night's rest and make an early start in the morning. As soon as we arrived home we set about loading up the bus with everything we needed. We were tired but we didn't want to be faced with the task in the morning. We had almost finished loading when I thought about checking the fuel. Throughout all the travelling we had done, and the strange events which kept happening, I had completely forgotten to keep an eye on the fuel situation. I switched on the ignition to check the gauge expecting it to read about half a tank, but to my surprise the needle was on the full mark. I tapped on the gauge thinking the needle was stuck. It didn't move so I gave it a sharp blow, but it didn't budge. I know faulty fuel gauges are pretty common, but they usually stick on empty. I thought quite reasonably the needle had jammed on full and the only way to test it was to try and dip the tank. As luck would have it, the filler tube to the tank was fairly straight. Had there been a bend in it I would have had difficulty in dipping it, but as it happened it was fairly straightforward to poke a long stick down it. I couldn't believe my eyes as I withdrew the stick and saw the tank was full. How could that be? By my estimation we had covered at least a hundred miles and yet the tank was brim full. I took a second dip only to confirm the same result. I didn't try to figure out how this could be. For a start I was too tired to think, and for another it was just another one of the many weird happenings we had encountered, and with the way things were going there was bound to be many more. When we were satisfied we had everything we needed, I suggested a night cap before we retired. I wanted us all to get a good night's sleep. It was a long journey and we all needed to be on full alert. It was as we sat about drinking and reflecting on the day's events, that Jason asked what the time was. I remember looking at him thinking what the on earth time had got to do with anything. When I considered what was going on, the time mattered not a jot.

"It must be getting on for eleven" I said.

"It must be after that," chimed Bill.

"At night?" asked Jason.

What is the matter with this lad? I thought. "Of course at night," I replied irritably.

"Well look out there," he said pointing through the window.

I was about to ask if he was cracking up, when it suddenly dawned on me what he was getting at. It was well into the night and yet it was still as bright as it had been all day. In fact, thinking about it, I can't remember it going dark at all since we surfaced from Hays Heath. It provided another twenty minutes of a talking point until I suggested we all get a good night's sleep, whether it was light or not.

I slept pretty soundly that night. Probably more to do with exhaustion than anything else, but on waking I felt surprisingly good and in a more refreshed state of mind. My brain, no doubt, was coming to terms with the situation. I kept telling myself it was no use panicking about our predicament, all we could do was search for the answer.

I rose from the bed, gave a mighty stretch and made for the bathroom. I showered and dressed and headed downstairs. I made straight for the kitchen to make my fix of coffee where I encountered Jason who proceeded to complain about tossing and turning all night and getting next to no sleep again. I offered to make him a coffee but he refused my offer. He followed me through to the living room blasting my eardrums about what was happening and when was it all going to end and why was it happening to him, as if he was the only one it was happening to. Unable to stand his moaning anymore, I asked him to go and wake Bill and Rod and ask them if they wanted breakfast before we left. It was a ploy to give me a bit of peace and quiet while I drank my coffee.

Jason was one of life's moaners. If there was a gold medal on offer at the Olympics for whiners, Jason would win it hands down. I did think it was because he was now not able to get hold of his supply of drugs, not that he was addicted, not yet anyway, but it was obvious to me, he needed them to calm himself down, or he would eventually crack up without them. Up until then I had kept those thoughts to myself, but I was toying with the idea of discussing them with Rod who was the closest to him.

9

At about 8-30 the next morning we were ready to leave, but before we did so Bill insisted I dip the fuel tank again. I reminded him I had dipped it the night before and that it was full to the brim. He just shook his head and said, "Funny things happen around here. You might find it empty now." I smiled at that statement, but had to admit to myself he was right. After all, we didn't want to get on the motorway and find out the petrol had now mysteriously disappeared. We needn't have worried however, as the dip revealed the tank was still full. I had long since given up wondering how this managed to be. I jumped back in the driver's seat and kicked up the engine. It was over two hundred miles to the capital so we had decided to take it in turns to drive.

I headed for the motorway which took us once again through Garton. I could have taken the by-pass but I was curious to have a last look just in case we had missed anything which would give us a vital clue as to what had happened. Nobody commented on my detour, they knew what was going through my head and were no doubt as curious as I was. Sadly it was as we expected it to be, but it didn't deter any of us from straining our eyes and craning our necks to catch some sign of movement.

Leaving Garton behind, I headed for the motorway. As I started to cross the bridge overlooking the six lane highway, I brought the bus gently to a halt and we all sat in silence gazing at the empty carriageways. A strange eerie feeling crept over me as I gazed at that ever narrowing road disappearing into a point in the distance. It was as though it was beckoning us to drive to that point, and once there we would all be swallowed into a black hole and never be seen again. I shrugged my shoulders and chided myself silently for thinking such nonsense, but even if that did happen, I told myself, it would be no different than the situation we were in now. However, I did at this point have a change of heart about travelling on the motorway, though I hasten to add, not for that reason. I thought it better we travel through as many built up areas as we could on our journey. It would take longer, but we didn't have a timetable to keep to, and this way we would satisfy ourselves that Garton was not the only town to have suffered the same fate. I expressed my views to the others who all agreed. I slipped the motor into gear and continued our journey.

The drive along the empty road was, for want of a better word, monotonous. I could have driven on the wrong side of the road if I had wanted to. There was nothing to be seen as mile after mile of desolate scenery passed by, only deserted farm buildings surrounded by empty fields and the occasional roadside houses forlornly waiting for their human owners to return to them.

After about sixty miles passing through silent villages and small towns, Bill pointed to a large roadside hotel we were approaching. He suggested I have a break from driving and the opportunity for all of us to stretch our legs. I pulled into a large deserted car park, making a joke that I would struggle to find a parking spot. Bill and Rod gave a broad smile which suggested to me they were now getting more relaxed about our predicament. I looked through the mirror at Jason. His head was flat against the window and in full sleep mode.

"Better wake him," said Rod. "If he wakes and we are not here, he will panic."

With that he gave him a gentle shake. There was no reaction, so he shook him a bit harder. Jason's eyes half flickered open. "What!" he said irritably.

"We're going to stretch our legs. Do you want to join us?"

"No. I'm ok," he grunted and closed his eyes and snuggled back down.

We left the bus and headed for the restaurant. Rod suddenly came to an abrupt halt.

"What is it?" asked Bill.

Rod pointed towards the restaurant. "It's him!"

"It's who?" I asked looking in the direction he was pointing.

"That … that thing whatever it is. He was by those doors staring at us."

"What thing?" asked Bill.

"You know the one which was on the T.V."

Bill and I looked to where he was pointing, but couldn't see anyone.

"Are you sure it wasn't our reflection in the glass?" asked Bill.

"No, no, it was him I tell you."

"Well, there's nobody there now," I said, but knowing Rod like I do, I knew he wasn't the sort given to wild imagination, so I was pretty sure he had seen something or thought he had, and given the strange goings on around us I wouldn't have been surprised to see the creature myself. At this point I suggested we take a quick scout around. After half an hour or so of searching and finding nothing, which was no surprise, we gave up the search. Bill peered into the dining room and wondered if there was any food about. Rod dismissed the idea saying "There's nobody about to make any, is there?" I suggested we take a look anyway, and made my way inside. Rod made a beeline for the kitchen. I stood there with Bill for a moment looking around. It was a fairly large dining room with thick red floral wall to wall carpet. There were about forty ample sized tables with high backed chairs to match. Large deep windows ran the length of one side of the room giving panoramic views of a river running close by. It was exquisitely decorated with expensive wallpaper complimenting the carpet. It was obviously a high class restaurant.

Rod's voice broke my concentration. He was standing by the kitchen door beckoning for us to go over to him. As we approached I could see his face was pale as though he'd had a shock. He just stared at me for a minute.

"What's the matter?" I said

"What's your favourite dish?" he asked.

I hesitated for a minute. The question had taken me completely by surprise. "My favourite dish? What are you talking about?"

"What's your favourite dish?" he repeated.

Bill looked at Rod, his face a picture of utter confusion "Are you ok Rod?" he asked.

"I'm perfectly fine thanks Bill. I'll explain in a minute, when Greg has answered my question."

"Roast beef, roast potatoes, sprouts and cauliflower with lashings of gravy, as you very well know," I answered.

Rod then turned to Bill. "And your favourite, Bill must be steak and kidney pie and chips."

Bill's Jaw dropped. "How on earth did you know that?"

Rod led us into the kitchen and pointed to the hot plates. "Look over there."

Neither Bill nor I could believe what we were seeing. On the hot plate were three steaming hot meals as though they had only just been prepared. Rod pointed to the other plate. "There's my favourite dish, grilled cod and salad done just how I like it. What do you think about that?"

I mumbled something about how it was getting weirder by the day, and who could have prepared our favourite dishes right before we appeared?

Rod was also quick to point out there were four of us but only three dishes of food were there. It was as though whoever or whatever had done this, had known that Jason would not be joining us.

Bill grabbed his plate. "I don't know about you lads," he said. "But at this very moment, I don't know and I don't care. I'm going to gobble this up before it disappears. I'll think about where it came from after."

Needless to say Rod and I followed his example, but there was another odd thing about this incident. As we carried our meals through the dining room, we came across a table which had been laid for three. After the meal we all had a quick wash and piled back onto the bus. Jason was still sound asleep, head right back on the headrest, his face pressed against the window and his breath creating a little patch of condensation on the glass, which appeared and disappeared with every inhale and exhale of breath. He had been oblivious of our little excursion, which was probably just as well. You could never tell from one minute to the next what state of mind he was going to be in, and I dreaded to think what he would have done if he had witnessed the goings on at the restaurant. He would have probably thought he was hallucinating. I was convinced his state of mind was the effects of his drug taking.

Bill had taken over the driving on the second part of our journey. We had agreed, for Jason's sake, there would be no mention of the restaurant incident. I took this as a sign we were all getting used to these unexplainable incidents, which was good in a way as there wasn't much danger of them now causing panic, Jason of course being the exception. On the other hand, I didn't want us to become so complacent with the situation and the strange events taking place that we took them for granted. To my way of thinking it may cause us to stop searching for the reason they were happening and give up looking for a solution.

Most of the time as the bus trundled along the roads there was complete silence, each of us stared out at the now familiar uninhabited landscape, eyes straining in the faint hope of catching a glimpse of movement. Bill kept a nice steady pace, ready to screech to a halt if any of us did manage to see anything. We virtually crawled through villages and small towns on our way, observing every window and doorway as we went, but as we had now come to expect, we left each village and town as abandoned as we had found them.

We pressed on for near enough another seventy miles before entering the spa town of Morchester, which had begun life as an early Roman settlement on the banks of the river Mor. It was originally a walled city, but it had long outgrown the confinement of its walls and was spreading rapidly in all directions. We headed for the town centre and cruised slowly around its inner core of narrow streets lined with gravity defying black and white timber framed buildings, before bringing the bus to a halt in the main shopping area.

We were getting used to the deafening silence and the deserted scene we were subjected to or perhaps it would be better to say we were getting a little more used to our predicament. Jason on the other hand, had no control over his emotions, and from time to time would verbally lash out at us, not that any of us took it to heart. We were all quite apprehensive about what was happening to us and wondered where and when it was all going to end, but for the sake of our sanity we had to keep our heads. Even so, every time I gazed upon the empty lifeless vista that confronted us everywhere we went, I felt as though I had somehow been imprisoned in a giant bubble and a feeling of claustrophobia would begin to descend. I would then have to quickly dismiss it from my mind and try and concentrate on trying to find an answer to all this. I was pretty sure Bill and Rod were also struggling with their emotions even though they fought hard to hide them from each other, especially Jason who would have gone to pieces if he had realised our true thoughts.

Our journey was slow because we had to navigate through some major towns and cities, and the fact that we were now about half-way to our destination, we decided to rest in Morchester for the night and try to find some food and lodgings. This was a tourist city so there was no shortage of hotels or restaurants. After touring the streets, we decided on a smart looking upmarket hotel. After all it wasn't going to cost us anything, was it?

We all made for the washrooms to freshen up and arranged to meet in the bar. After a quick drink we decided to find the restaurant. As we entered the room, Rod gave Bill a wink and suggested he and Jason grab a table, while he and I searched the kitchen for something to eat. Bill was quick to cotton on and guided Jason to a table.

"What would you like, Jason?" asked Rod.

"Very funny," grunted Jason. "How are you going to get food? There's no one about, is there?"

"You never know," answered Rod. "There was food on the shelves and in the freezers at the last place we stopped."

"Ok. I'll have a hamburger with fried onions. How about that?"

By now I had cottoned on to what Rod was up to, and was impressed with his quick thinking with regards as to what had happened the last time when we found meals already waiting. We didn't know if there was going to be a recurrence of that here, but I suppose he was taking the precautionary measure of keeping Jason out of the kitchen in case it did. He obviously thought, that with Jason's delicate mental state, an occurrence like this would have sent him over the top.

"That's your favourite is it Jason?" I asked.

"It sure is," he replied. "In fact you can make it two."

Rod couldn't help but smile. "I'll see what I can do."

Rod and I entered the kitchen together. We weren't disappointed, if that is how you can phrase such a weird phenomenon, because there on the hot plates were our four favourite meals. Not wanting to rush straight out with them and be questioned by Jason as to how we had managed to conjure up four meals so quickly, we hung around in the kitchen for a while. In fact it had given me the perfect opportunity to voice my concerns about Jason's state of mind and his drug habit.

Rod's answers to my questions were not exactly reassuring. "I've tried to get him to break the habit without much success," he said. "I've talked to him until I'm blue in the face, but I'm afraid he thinks his past misdemeanours are about to catch up with him and this is his way of blotting it from his mind. I haven't given up on him, but I'm sorry to say, I think he's on a downward spiral. If he could stop now before it gets too bad, he will have a fighting chance, but now all this has happened I fear the worst. He's not going to stop with all this going on, is he?" I pointed out that if he was hungry enough to eat two hamburgers, then perhaps he was improving. Rod shook his head. "I wouldn't bet on him eating them," he said. "I'll be surprised if he eats one of them never mind both. I've seen him order food like this before and then thrown most of it away."

We picked up the meals and took them through to where they were sitting and set them down on the table. "There we are Jason," said Rod. "How about these?"

Jason looked at the hamburgers. "They look very nice," he said, but made no movement to pick them up. Not the reaction you would expect from someone who had eaten hardly anything all day. Rod's main priority at this point was to try and get some food into him and urged him to "Get stuck in." Jason reached out with the speed of a Sloth and took a small bite and immediately put the hamburger back on the plate, announcing he wanted to go to the washroom. As he disappeared through the door, Rod turned to me with a told you so look on his face. "See what I mean?" he said. "I knew he wouldn't eat it. He's probably gone in there for a snort."

"Then we have to stop him," I urged, turning to make for the washroom, but Rod grabbed me by the arm and stopped me in my tracks.

"That won't do any good," he said. "I've tried that tact. I've spent time at his flat to try and stop him using the stuff but it didn't work, in fact he had the gall to try and get me on it. I've tried reasoning with him to get him to see the error of his ways. I've even tried the opposite way by lecturing him, but it just made things worse."

"You'll just have to leave him to it," announced Bill. "If he isn't going to listen to anybody there's nothing you can do about it."

Rod sighed deeply at Bill's forthright statement. "Well, I haven't given up on him yet," he replied.

I thought that a bold statement, but both Bill and I noticed a hint of resignation in his voice. I couldn't help but feel sorry for Rod; he had evidently gone out of his way to help this seemingly ungrateful lad, only to get snubbed for his pains. As far as I was concerned Jason was a lost cause and Rod was wasting his breath on him. The truth is, I simply haven't got the patience with anyone who will not help themselves. I had gone through all this with Sylvia and I wasn't going to go through a repeat performance. I couldn't help thinking Bill had also lost patience with Jason too.

After the meal, we each selected a bedroom each, and taking a nice refreshing shower, I closed the heavy drapes to keep out that permanent daylight, and threw myself onto the inviting king sized bed.

10

The human mind is a strange thing. I don't think anyone will ever figure out how it really works. I say this, because as I awoke the next morning, I had my eyes tightly shut but my brain was already processing my very first thought. I was hoping it had all been a dream and when I opened my eyes I would be in my own bedroom in my own house. I slowly forced open my eyelids. You can imagine the disappointment at finding nothing had changed. I washed and dressed and made my way down to the dining room. Bill and Rod were already there. "I could do with some of that," I said pointing to Bill's plate of bacon and eggs.

"It will come as no surprise to tell you it was ready and waiting," he grinned. "Just help yourself."

I trotted off to the kitchen and returned with my plate piled high. I wasn't a big eater during the day, but I did enjoy a hearty breakfast. As I was about to make short work of my perfectly cooked breakfast, the door swung open and a bleary eyed Jason entered the room. I pointed to my plate but he screwed up his face and quickly dismissed the idea with a wave of his hand.

Rod poured him a strong coffee. "This is his idea of breakfast," he said, pushing the steaming cup of coffee towards him.

Jason gave an enormous yawn and lowered himself on to his seat. "What's happening today then?" he asked.

The three of us just looked at each other. "What sort of question is that?" Grunted Bill. "We are heading for London. Battersea Power Station, you know we are."

Jason never looked up from his coffee. "Yes, I do know that, but what's the plan when we get there?"

Rod could see Bill's face colour up and quickly interrupted the conversation. "There isn't a plan when we get there, Jason. Because we don't know what we are going to find, do we?"

"I don't think you are going to find anything there," he mumbled, sipping his coffee. "It's going to be no different than here, is it?"

"So what would you do then, Jason my lad?" spat Bill. "What would your plan be?"

Bill's angry tone made Jason look up from his coffee. "Well...err...I err..."

"You haven't got a clue, have you lad?" snapped Bill. "I'm getting sick and tired of you sitting back and letting everybody else do the thinking, then moaning and groaning because you think it's wrong. If you had some input into what we were doing instead of sneaking off and pumping drugs into yourself then you might know what is going on. I'll tell you this for nothing, son. If you carry on the way you are doing, you will be left behind to fend for yourself. You are of no use to any of us the way you are." There followed a stunned silence. We were all taken aback at Bill's sudden aggressiveness. I think anger at Jason's negative attitude had been building up like a pressure cooker in Bill for a while and Jason's attitude this morning was the last straw. Jason suddenly banged his cup on the table and stormed out.

"I think perhaps you were a bit over the top, Bill," said Rod.

"Over the top!" roared Bill. "If you ask me I wasn't *hard* enough on him. You are too soft with him, Rod. He needs a wake-up call. We don't need passengers like him. I meant what I said. If he doesn't start pulling his weight, he is going to get left behind." I had to back Bill up. I pointed out, that in his present state, Jason was a danger not only to himself but to all of us.

Rod rose from his chair. "I suppose you are right. I think it's about time he pulled his weight. I would like to have a few words with him before we set off."

Whatever Rod had said to Jason it seemed to have stopped his constant moaning, for now at least, but his sullen mood remained. An hour later we were on the road again with Rod now in the driving seat. Hardly a word passed between us as we wound our way towards London. By now we were all used to the desolate scene passing us by and we had exhausted all our questions and answers. Jason was as usual fast asleep, this time stretched out across the rear seats. I unfolded a route map and studied it, more for want of something else to think about other than the situation we were in. By my reckoning we had done no more than thirty miles, when, as we negotiated the brow of a hill, Rod brought the bus to a halt. He jumped from the bus and pointed down the valley. "Look," he said excitedly. "It looks as though there is life there. I can see movement."

Bill and I scrambled from the bus and stared at what appeared to be a sizeable town. I reached inside the bus and grabbed the map. I checked and double checked that map against our present location. "That's strange," I said. "According to this map there is no town here."

"Well, it's there," said Rod pointing towards it. "And what is more there appears to be life in the place. There must be something wrong with the map."

I was about to say the map was barely twelve months old, but I thought better of it. The town was there and there was no doubt about that. We piled back into the vehicle and headed at breakneck speed towards it. We noticed that while the sky above us still had that yellow haze about it, there was a cloudless blue circle above the town. I thought it odd too, as we approached the town, that we could clearly see people going about their business, and traffic making its way along the streets, but none of it was actually entering or leaving the conurbation. Then strangely, about thirty yards before the boundary, which was marked with a signpost announcing we were about to enter the town of Woldsmere, the engine spluttered and died. Rod had several attempts to re-start it but it stubbornly refused.

"It looks as though the petrol has finally run out," sighed Rod. I asked him what the gauge reading said. "It's reading full like it always does," He replied. "But that means nothing, does it?"

I grabbed my stick and dipped the tank. It came as no surprise to me to find the tank full to the brim. I suggested the engine may have overheated and would be best to leave it to cool down while we walked into town. Jason was already heading in that direction.

"Don't go wandering off, Jason," Rod shouted after him. "Let's all stick together."

"Calm down," replied Jason. "Nothing's happened to these people has it? So it's quite safe."

"Do as Jason says, lad," growled Bill. "It might not be safe. You know how things happen around here."

"Oh stop worrying," he shouted back, and turned and strode forward. As he drew level with the sign, there was a blinding flash of lightning. It was a couple of moments before our eyes had adjusted. We could see that Jason had disappeared. While Bill and I stood rooted to the spot trying to take in what had happened, Rod rushed forward to where Jason was last seen. I shouted for him to stop where he was, but as he told me later, in his concern for Jason, common sense was left behind. As he reached the spot where Jason had been, there was another blinding flash and he also vanished. Paralysed with a mixture of shock and disbelief, Bill and I stood looking at each other.

"What the heck is happening?" cried Bill. I confessed I hadn't got a clue but insisted we must find out what had happened to them. Bill gave me a long hard stare. "What! You mean... follow them to that spot?"

I looked at Bill for what seemed a lifetime. His face was the colour of whitewash. I nodded meekly and I could feel my face drain of blood. I was scared to death, but what was the alternative. How could we possibly turn our backs on Jason and Rod not knowing what had happened. There was no way I was going to go on without them. There was only one answer to give, we both knew that. "Yes," I replied in a hoarse whisper.

Bill was certain Rod and Jason could not have survived that lightning blast and said we would suffer the same fate if we went near the same spot. "I don't think they are dead," I said. "I don't think whoever or whatever is controlling this, wants us dead."

"Controlling us?" he snapped back at me. "What are you talking about? You think someone is controlling us? I think you are losing it Greg."

"Ok," I said. "Explain to me how we managed to go back in time. Explain the continual full tank of petrol. Explain the meals ready for us, and if you don't believe that thing on the television is pointing us in the direction of Battersea Power Station for a reason, why are you with us?"

Bill shrugged his shoulders. "I suppose there is something to what you say, and I sure would like to find out what's going on."

"Then we have no alternative," I said. "We have to find out what has happened to Rod and Jason." Reluctantly, Bill agreed. I suggested we fill a couple of haversacks with food and drink before we take the plunge, "You never know what you are going to find, or what situation we may find ourselves in," I said.

We approached the area nervously and stopped a couple of feet from the sign. I was shaking with fear and broke out in a nervous sweat. My heart was pounding so hard I thought it was going to burst through my chest at any minute, and I assumed from Bill's laboured breathing, he was feeling this way too. "We have to do this together," I said. Counting to three, and with arms around each other like a couple of lovers, we stepped beyond the sign. There was a mighty flash. It could have only lasted a few seconds, but in that time I thought my eardrums were going to explode and my body burst into flames. I found myself sprawled out on the roadway next to Bill. My first instinct was to check myself out to make sure there were no serious injuries like a missing like a leg or an arm. I had a bit of a headache and my ears were ringing, but apart from that, neither of us had as much as a scratch. We hauled ourselves to our feet and dusted ourselves down. There was no sign of Jason and Rod.

"What do you think has happened to them?" asked Bill.

I presumed the same thing had happened to them as it did with us and they had escaped unharmed, otherwise they would have still been there, and knowing Rod as I do, I guessed his inquisitive streak had kicked in, and he would have gone off to explore the town knowing we would follow, because that is what he would have done had it been us who had disappeared. I guessed the best place to head for would be the centre of town, so we made our way there.

I checked out my watch. There was no particular reason for it; it didn't really matter what time it was. It was a habit of mine checking the time every now and then. I was disappointed though to see it had stopped. I assumed at the time it was caused by the static created when we penetrated the wall. I made no mention of it to Bill because it mattered not in the scheme of things.

We started to make our way along the street, which, as we had observed earlier, was fairly busy with traffic, but where it was going to and coming from being a mystery. My suspicions were aroused about this place when, as I watched a vehicle drive by us heading towards the edge of town, it suddenly disappeared as it reached a certain point. Just as suddenly, another vehicle appeared from nowhere travelling towards us. Again I made no mention of it to Bill. He hadn't noticed this occurrence, so I thought it best not to bring it to his attention. One thing we both noticed though, was that we had to sidestep anyone we met coming in the opposite direction or they would have barged straight into us.

"What's the matter with these people?" commented Bill. "Have they all got bad eyesight?"

We continued on towards the centre. Then we heard someone shout. I looked along the street and spotted Rod and Jason waving to us. We made our way to them.

"What do you make of this place then?" asked Rod.

I knew immediately something was not right. I know Rod, he wouldn't have asked a question like that if there wasn't something to it.

Bill was unaware of the vibes Rod was giving off. "It's fantastic," he said. "Life at last."

"I'm not so sure," I said. "At first glance everything appears normal, but it can't be right, can it?"

"What do you mean by that?" asked Bill.

"Look at the facts," I answered. "For three days all we have seen is a deserted world. Then all of a sudden we see a town going about its business as though everything was normal. They seem completely unaware the rest of humanity has vanished.

"Well they are here," grunted Bill, pointing towards the people scurrying to and fro. "Right in front of your eyes. There's no getting away from that is there?"

"Go and speak to one of them," grinned Rod. "Ask them what town this is."

"Excuse me," said Bill to an approaching woman. She completely ignored him and just carried on walking, not even glancing at him. "Excuse me," he shouted to a man as he drew level. "I just want to know where we are." Again the man walked on, oblivious to Bill. "They must have seen me," he growled what is the matter with them?"

"They can't see you," commented Rod.

"But I'm standing almost in front of them," he said. "There's something wrong here."

"You bet there's something wrong," grumbled Jason.

"What are you guys on about?" asked Bill, a look of confusion spread across his face.

"We are not supposed to be here," answered Rod "The place isn't real,"

"Isn't real!" spluttered Bill. "What do you mean, isn't real?"

"Look, let me show you." Rod moved to the edge of the pavement, and as a car approached, he stepped in front of it. Bill and I gave a look of horror and made a lunge to stop him, but it was too late, the car had no chance of avoiding him. I couldn't believe my eyes at what happened next. The car had passed straight through him. Rod simply walked back to join us.

I saw Bill's knees buckle and he sank down onto a nearby bench. The blood had drained from his face and his mouth agape–swearing and cursing. I must admit, although I was expecting something like that because of what Rod had said, it was a hair raising moment for me too, although not as traumatic as it was for Bill. I glanced over to Jason. I knew he wouldn't be very happy about the situation and when he saw me looking at him, it prompted an expected outburst from him.

"I knew it!" he raved. "I might have known it was too good to be true. So what are we supposed to do now?"

Rod fixed him with a poker faced stare. "We carry on with our original plan," he answered in a very matter of fact tone. Jason averted his eyes from Rod's glare and fell quiet. The look on Rod's face enough to silence him.

"I don't understand what's going on here," uttered Bill. "Are they ghosts?"

"It is us who are the ghosts, Bill," Responded Rod. "Not them."

Bill looked profoundly shocked at that statement. "Us, ghosts! What makes you say that?"

"Well, this may sound weird, but…"

"I don't suppose it's going to sound any more weird than what we have seen up to now," interrupted Bill.

"I think you will all agree by now," resumed Rod. "That by some fluke we have all gone back in time, and as there is nothing to go by, I can't tell how far back we have gone. Looking at the vehicles here though, and the design of the clothes being worn, I would say this is about the same year it was before we were transported back. On that theory, I think we have entered some sort of time warp."

"Well I can't think of a better explanation," I said "What about you, Bill and Jason?"

The only reaction we had off those two, was a "Suppose so" from Bill and a shrug of the shoulders from Jason, who confessed it was all way over his head.

"Well, it's no use standing about here," urged Rod. "We might as well get on our way."

We immediately made our way to the edge of town. As we neared the signpost indicating the town boundary, I gave a cautionary warning to be careful, reminding everyone of the dramatic entrance we had made. We came to a halt about ten yards from the signpost and stood looking at each other, none of us wanting to be the first to cross.

Bill was the first to volunteer. "I'm going to take a run at it he said. I think it will be the best way. That way I will not have time to think about it." Without any more hesitation he ran towards the boundary and gave a flying leap. There was a blinding flash. When our eyes recovered, Bill was lying a few yards away, perfectly still. With heart pounding I rushed to Bill's side followed by Rod and Jason. Thankfully, Bill was just winded and was just as shocked to see us as we were him. "What on earth happened?" he gasped.

I confessed I hadn't a clue why he hadn't reached the other side, and neither could Rod offer an explanation. We sat there thinking for a moment.

Then Rod stood to his feet staring at the boundary. I knew he had an idea.

"This may be a totally stupid idea," he said. "Why don't we try the same sequence going out as we did when we came in."

"You mean Jason first, then you, then me and Bill together. I think that's well worth a try," I said.

I could have bet on Jason's reaction. "Me, first?" he yelled. "No way. I'm not going first. Look what happened to Bill."

Bill stood to his feet, his face contorted with anger. "Now look here you snivelling little wimp. If it wasn't for you we wouldn't be in this mess. Do you want to get out of here or not? Now you either try it voluntary or I will pick you up and throw you at it. What do you want it to be?"

From the look on Bill's face, Jason reckoned he had no choice. "Ok. Ok, I'll give it a go." He stood for a moment plucking up courage, then suddenly he shot off towards the boundary, taking Bill's advice to take a running jump at it. Again there was a tremendous flash with the same result as Bill's try. He was flung back towards us. We raced to him, but apart from being a bit shaken up he was unhurt. None of us spoke for a minute. I suppose we were all a bit taken aback by what had happened, I know I was.

Bill was the first to break the silence, uttering the question which was on everyone's lips. "At the risk of sounding like Jason," he grunted sarcastically. "What now?"

"We got in here, so why can't we get out?" growled Jason. "We are stuck in here now, aren't we? We are going to die in here, trapped like rats in a cage."

"Hush, Jason," spat Rod. "Panicking will get us nowhere. It's time to put our thinking caps on."

As Rod was more into this science stuff than any of us, I had an idea I wanted to put to him. "You say this is a time warp, Rod?"

"Yes," he replied. "It's a sort of bubble that floats about in the fabric of time like you can get an air bubble in the atmosphere. You must have been on a plane when it has encountered an air pocket. The plane suddenly drops because it is in effect a vacuum bubble. This is the same, except this is a bubble of time that floats about space. Why, what are you thinking?"

"Well, we obviously got in here, so there must be a weakness in it somewhere. Perhaps we are not at the exact spot."

"Of course!" cried Rod. "Why didn't I think of it before? You are right in thinking there may be a weakness, Greg. Only it's not a weakness as such, but a door or portal as it is known. The problem is, they move about, what we have to do is find that portal."

"How do we do that?" I asked.

"There is only one way, and that is to walk the boundary and keep touching the wall until we do find it."

"I'm not touching that thing again," yelled Jason.

"I don't mean with our bare hands." Rod Growled. "We have to get something to touch it with."

"I don't want to sound negative," I said. "But how are we going to do that? Nothing here is solid."

Rod, scratched at the back of his head. "Yes I see what you mean."

"We've got these," cried Bill pointing to his belt. "We could swing these at it."

We all took off our belts. "What's the plan?" I said.

"The quickest way," answered Rod. "Would be for two to travel in one direction and two to go in the opposite direction, but I am reluctant to do that in this situation. I think it best if we all stuck together." We all nodded agreement. In this uncertain environment none of us wanted to lose sight of each other in case something should happen to any of us.

"Let's space out at ten yard intervals, that way we shouldn't miss any of the wall. Swing your belts buckle first at the wall, if it flashes and bounces straight back carry on. If it flashes and doesn't bounce back, we have found the portal. Let's go."

We trekked around the boundary swinging away with our belts for what seemed hours. Finally, through sheer exhaustion, we found an open grassed area and collapsed to the ground. Bill and I opened the haversacks we had brought and dished out the welcome food and drink, with a warning we must eke out the supplies seeing as we didn't know how long we were going to be stuck there.

"Be honest, Rod," said Bill. "What are the chances of finding this portal thing, or whatever it is you call it?"

Rod shrugged his shoulders. "Well, I'll have to say the chance of finding it is very slim. There will be a portal for certain, but it could be anywhere. It may not even be at this level, it could be well out of our reach by now." He pointed to the sky. "It may well be floating about up there. I think it was pure coincidence we stumbled across it when we did."

"I knew it," barked Jason. "We are going to die here aren't we?"

"And whose fault is it we are in this mess?" snapped Bill. "If you hadn't ignored our advice and gone wandering off, we wouldn't be in this predicament."

"Now come on boys," I pleaded. "It's no good shouting at each other. It isn't going to help matters. As for you Jason, for goodness sake pull yourself together. It's a good job the rest of us don't give up so easily. We just have to keep looking. Now I suggest we get some rest before we continue."

I must have fallen asleep almost immediately, and it must have been a deep sleep because the next thing I knew Rod was shaking me. "Come on Greg, time to move. I want to get as far as I can before it gets dark, to which I pointed out it had never gone dark since we came up from the mine. He seemed to ignore that statement and looked around at the others who were still asleep. He put his face close to mine and whispered, "I didn't want the other two to hear this, especially Jason, but these time bubbles never stay in one place. I reckon this one will be on the move before long, so we have to find the portal if we can before it does. If it does move before we find it, then it won't matter anymore whether we find it or not, because we may find ourselves trapped in another completely different time zone."

I sprang to my feet. "Then we had better get moving," I said.

We awakened Bill and Jason. Rod plausibly telling them with the portal moving about we shouldn't delay in searching for it or it may disappear altogether. I almost believed it myself. After tramping for hours and resting when we could, we had finally completed the circle without success. Rod and I realised now we had been unable to find the portal, and were never liable to do so, it was inevitable we were trapped in this time warp and would be transported with it wherever it wanted to go.

Nothing was said by anyone. If there were questions to be asked, we were all too exhausted to ask them. All we wanted to do now was to sleep, and sleep we did, anywhere we could find a comfortable spot. Questions would have to wait until later.

11

I was awoken by Bill, who was standing over me repeatedly shouting my name. For a couple of minutes I couldn't for the life of me think where I was or what was going on. I had been having a vivid dream about Sylvia, and how, in that dream, we were so in love and living life to the full, so I was not a happy man to find Bill's face looking down at me and not Sylvia's. By this time Rod had joined him.

Bill pointed to the sky. I shielded my eyes from the glare. The sky was as clear and blue as it had been since we had arrived, but now lightning flashes were dancing across it, getting more violent with every flash.

"What do you think is going on, Rod?" I asked.

"I'm only guessing," he answered. "But I think the bubble is about to move."

I remembered what Rod had told me about what the consequences would be if it did move. I felt a huge knot tighten in my stomach. I don't mind telling you I was beginning to panic. "We have to do something," I cried. "I don't want to end up trapped in a bubble floating about in different time zones."

"I've got an idea," he said. "But we have to hurry."

"What's going on?" Bill shouted to Rod.

I'll explain later," he replied. "Just grab Jason and run for the boundary."

Bill shook Jason awake, and without saying a word, he hauled him to his feet.

"What's going on?" asked the bewildered Jason.

"Never mind," yelled Bill. "Just run."

Rod led the way as we all ran as fast as we could to the boundary with the lightning increasing in intensity. We came to a halt a few feet from the boundary. Rod instructed us to link arms. "This may not work but it's worth a try. I want us all to keep together and get as close to the edge of the bubble as possible. This thing is going to disappear, and just before it does I want us all to fling ourselves at the wall."

"But it will throw us back in, won't it?" Bill asked.

"Not if we time it right. These lightning strikes are weakening the walls, which is why it uproots itself and moves on. We have to time it right, so when it's at its weakest and is ready to move we have to jump through and hope the wall is weak enough for us to penetrate it."

"How are we going to know when the time is right?" I asked.

"Leave that to me," replied Rod. "Now grip each other firmly and line up near the wall. I will tell you when, but we must all jump together as one unit."

We moved as close to the wall as we could. The bubble wall was now visible as hundreds of veins of lightning coursed through it and I could feel it pulling me towards it. The lightning was getting ever more ferocious and the static played around us, lifting my hair almost on end. The air was now filled with a continuous crescendo of ear splitting   noises. Then came the mightiest bang of all. A massive lightning bolt shot past our heads and into the wall

"NOW!" yelled Rod at the top of his voice. "NOW!"

With perfect timing we all launched ourselves at the wall. I could remember a halo of static surrounding me. The acrid smell of electricity like that of a shorting battery filled my nostrils and the noise was horrendous.

Greg suddenly stopped relating his story and turned to me. "Do you remember the lightning incident a while ago?" he asked.

"Yes quite clearly," I answered.

"Well, this was the cause of my panic that day. I was scared to death of it being a repeat of this incident and being flung back into another time warp." Greg continued with the story. "The next thing I knew as I came around, was finding myself sprawled face down on the ground, my body throbbing in places I didn't know I had. My head was aching and my eyes were sore and there was a tremendous ringing in my ears. Gathering all the strength I could muster, I raised myself to a sitting position. My immediate thought was to check to see if we had we escaped the warp. I heaved a huge sigh of relief when I saw there were no more lightning bolts and the town had disappeared. I looked about me to see the others sprawled out across the ground and the bus was exactly where we had left it. As if by command the others began to stir. I hauled myself to my feet and made my way towards them.

Bill rose shakily to his feet. "We made it then," he said.

"Thanks to this man here," I said pointing to Rod.

Rod grinned. "Well, I must say it was a calculated risk, I'm just glad it worked."

"We're still in a mess though, aren't we?"

We all turned to see Jason's scowling face. I could see Bill's face reddening with anger. He made a move towards him. "You ungrateful lit…"

I caught his arm to prevent him going any further. "Forget it Bill," I said. "It isn't worth it." Although having said that, I could willingly have smacked Jason myself.

Bill snatched his arm out of my grip and stormed off towards the bus. He wasn't the only one whose patience with Jason was beginning to wear a little thin. Rod glared at him and pointed an angry finger at him.

"If you don't want to be with us and you think you can do better, then we will part company now and you can go it alone. If you want to remain in our company, I suggest you keep your mouth shut until you can come up with any sensible ideas instead of moaning and groaning all the time, the choice is yours." I think Jason was too stunned by Rod's verbal lashing to respond directly. He just stood there not believing Rod had spoken to him like that. "Well!" snapped Rod. "What's it to be?"

"I… err. I… err. I'm coming with you."

"Ok, but don't forget what I have told you. And keep away from Bill until he has cooled down. Now let's get on our way." He turned to me. "Do you think we will make it to London today, Greg?"

I automatically looked at my watch ready to give an answer, forgetting it had been damaged crashing through the bubble wall. I stared at it for a minute as I could see the second finger was moving. Then I held it to my ear. It was ticking away as normal. Rod asked what the matter was. "How long were we in the time warp bubble?" I asked.

"A day at least," he answered. "Maybe longer, why?"

"My watch has started again," I said. "But it's showing yesterday's date and the time we entered the time warp, plus about twenty minutes."

Rod looked at me for a minute then nodded. "Of course," he said. "There is no time in those warps, so our watches would have appeared to stop. They would start again once we got out."

"So we are just a day out," I said.

Rod shook his head. "No. You see time would have been at a standstill all the while we were in there. This is the same time and the same day we went in, plus the twenty minutes we spent recovering. Follow me, I'll prove it."

We made our way to the bus. "He pointed to the clock. Take a look," he said.

He was right. The clock on the bus showed the exact time as my watch. I shook my head. All this time travel and time warps were way over my head. I just took Rod's word for it. "Come on," I said. "Let's get going. Who is in the driving seat?" Rod suggested Bill drove. He thought a spell behind the wheel, concentrating on the driving, would take his mind off his altercation with Jason for a while.

We eventually made it to the outskirts of London. I looked at my watch. It was showing 8.15, but since there was no indication as to where the sun was and no sunrise or sunset to go by, I could only guess it was evening, not that it made any difference, time was irrelevant. We were all hungry and tired so we decided we would find a place to eat and sleep and continue on into the capital when we were refreshed.

It was no surprise anymore to find our meals ready and waiting, even though we had picked the hotel at random. In fact we were so used to this phenomenon; we actually had the temerity to moan about having the same meals each time. That's human nature for you, isn't it?

My watch showed 7.35 as I awoke from a deep and surprisingly refreshing sleep. I washed and dressed and made my way down to the kitchens. It looked as though I was the first to breakfast as all four meals were ready and waiting as usual. I picked up my overflowing plate and made my way through to the dining room. I was about to tuck in when the door was flung open and Rod walked in followed by Bill. They marched off to the kitchens and reappeared with their respective meals. Jason of course was the last to appear. There wasn't a lot said over breakfast, but eventually Rod spoke.

"I don't know about you lads," he said. "But I think this is the day we are going to find out what all this is about."

"I'm with you on that score, Rod," I said. "I have a gut feeling we are going to catch up with whatever that was on the television. He kept pointing to Battersea Power Station, so I think it will all come to a head there."

"What will?" grunted Jason.

"We don't know, do we?" answered Rod. "But there must be some reason why all this is happening to us. I think we are about to find out."

After breakfast we piled into the bus. I decided to drive us on what we hoped would be the last leg of the journey. I knew exactly where Battersea Power Station was, I had driven past it several times on my visits to London.

Before we started though, I decided, out of curiosity, to dip the fuel tank. It was full of course, I never really expected it wouldn't be, but it was something I just couldn't get out of my mind.

We drove through the lifeless city streets getting nearer to our goal. It was the eeriest of feelings looking out onto this huge now desolate metropolis. It was still hard to take in, like living in a twilight zone. The world's greatest tourist attractions. Trafalgar square, Buckingham Palace, Piccadilly Circus, all completely deserted. We crawled along Oxford Street and Regent Street whose thoroughfares would normally be the busiest shopping streets in Britain, but now they, like everywhere else, presented an empty and desolate scene. It was only now that the full reality hit us like a ton of bricks. Until now we had hoped and prayed that here at least, in one of the biggest cities in the world, we would probably find more people in the same situation as we were, and who might provide an answer to what was going on. I will admit I felt despair on looking out at that mind numbing scene, and though not a word was spoken by anyone, I could also see it etched on the others faces as they too stared out on to this abandoned city.

We headed for the River Thames and along the road that ran beside it. Suddenly as we rounded a bend we sighted our goal. There it was, that huge red brick building with its four towering chimneys standing out proudly across the river as though guarding the south bank of the Thames. I had seen this Colossus of a building a few times and it always gave me a funny feeling in the pit of my stomach each time. This time though my stomach did a complete flip. We had travelled many miles to get here, and now there it was, a building of such majesty, you felt as though you had to bow to it. I pulled to the side of the road and we all just sat in silence gazing at the awe inspiring building, wondering just what was in store for us.

"I don't like it," cried Jason. "Let's not go in there."

"I don't know about you boys," I said. "I am not turning back now."

"Rod agreed with me. "We've come this far. We might as well see what it's all about."

There was no hesitation from Bill either. "I'm with you boys, he said. "There's no point in travelling all this way just to turn back now."

"I don't like it," scowled Jason. "We don't know what we are getting into, do we?"

Rod was very calm and collected as he turned to face Jason. How he managed to keep his cool was beyond me, but cool he was. "I know you are frightened, Jason," he said. "We all are. If the truth were known we would all like to get out of here, but where would we go? There is nowhere to go is there? We are trapped in a deserted world in which we have no hope of surviving. At least we ought to go and see why that creature has brought us here. It may be our only way back to normality. You can stay if you like, but the rest of us are going on. I would like us all to stick together, but the choice is yours."

Our eyes were now fixed on Jason, who was sitting perfectly still, staring at the larger than life power station. His face was pale and drawn, his reddened eyes now filling with tears. "Do you think we will ever get back?" he asked, wiping away the tears with the back of his hand.

As much as I had berated him over the last few days, and there were times I would have willingly left him behind, I couldn't help but feel sorry for the lad. Rod put a comforting arm around him. "Of course we'll get back. I think that is what this is all about. We can't stop now, can we?"

Finally Jason gave a nod of the head, which was the signal for me to engage gear and head over the bridge towards the huge complex. We sped down the power station approach road heading into the realms of the unknown. As we neared the huge iron gates which guarded a massive expanse of concreted yard, they swung slowly open unaided. As I nudged the vehicle through those towering iron structures, we all became gripped with a deepening feeling of trepidation. Cold sweats of fear were appearing on our faces. You may be frightened, terrified at facing an enemy you can see, but when you are confronting the unknown, that fear becomes an unbearable dread. Your pulse races at an unbelievable rate. Your heart pounds against your chest and any minute you think it is going to burst from your ribs.

I pulled to a stop just inside the gates. I was trembling all over. I had to grip the steering wheel as hard as I could to stop my hands shaking violently. I was fearful of going any further into the complex. We sat for what seemed an eternity, our eyes darting back and forth for any sign of life.

"Look," yelled Jason, making us jump out of our skin, "Over there." We all looked in the direction of where he was pointing a wavering finger. "There," he cried. "Standing by that big green door."

"It's that thing," said Rod. "There was no mistaking him. He's beckoning to us.

"What do you think?" asked Bill.

I was scared witless and admitted it. "Well, this is why we came," I said, trying to sound calm and collected. I didn't give the others the opportunity to discuss it. I engaged gear and made towards him. I say him, because none of us could figure out just what it was. It wasn't human and that's for sure. I stopped about five yards from him and kept the engine ticking over as a precaution.

He beckoned for us to approach him. I automatically switched off the engine and we all climbed from the bus and walked towards him. He stood there for a few moments staring at us. I can still feel those big almond shaped yellow eyes examining me now, which he seemed to do to each of us in turn. I couldn't call it hypnosis, but I was unable to break away from that penetrating stare. In that few moments though, the terrible feeling of dread had completely disappeared from all of us, including Jason. For the first time since all this began, all our deep set fears and frustration at failing to resolve our nightmare situation was gone. Complete calm and peacefulness had descended on us. I had no doubt it was the creatures doing.

He pointed a long bony finger at the big green door, which again, unaided, had swung slowly open. He waved us inside where we were confronted by another set of doors. The outer door closed shut trapping us between the two. Under normal circumstances this would probably have triggered a panic attack by one or all of us, but surprisingly we felt nothing but calm.

Then I heard a voice in my head, we all did. The creature was talking but his lipless mouth wasn't moving. He told us he went by the name of Zull and we were not to be afraid. He said he knew all about the past history of each of us and had brought us here to help us if we desired it, but at this point we were free to leave any time.

We looked at each other somewhat bewildered. I don't think for one moment any of us questioned how he knew all about our past lives. Oddly enough we all took it for granted that this was the case, but what did cross my mind was, what did he want to help us with? The others must have been thinking the same thing because again Zull's voice filled our heads.

"I see you are confused as to how we can help you." He pointed to the inner door. "To fully explain, you will need to enter beyond this portal. However, it is only one way. Once you have entered, the only way out is to take part in the programme or by permission of the operator. Once again there is nothing to be afraid of. I can assure you, this programme will be of great benefit to all of you, but the choice is yours. If you decide you want to leave now, you will be free to do so and your memories of this place will be erased. What is your choice?"

We looked at each other for a minute. "I'm going for it," I said. "What is the alternative?"

Rod pointed to the door through which we had just entered. "Well there's nothing out there, what have we got to lose?"

"I don't think we have a choice, do we?" sighed Bill.

We all looked at Jason. He was obviously in a state of confusion. He kept glancing behind him at the door we had just entered by. "I'm not sure about this," he said. He pointed to the door ahead. "We don't know what is through there, do we?"

"No we don't," I said. "But we do know what is through there, don't we?" I pointed to the door by which we had just entered. "Nothing only a deserted lifeless world that is what is through that door. Now the rest of us are going ahead. It is up to you."

Jason didn't hesitate. "I'll have to go with you guys. I'm not going back on my own."

Zull pointed to the inner door which disappeared before our eyes to be replaced by a green shimmering curtain of light. "Please enter."

Almost simultaneously we stepped into that shimmering light. What I saw before me when we emerged from that curtain of light made me gasp with astonishment. The sheer size of the space we had entered took my breath away. It was as though we had been transported into the vast emptiness of space. There were no visible walls or ceiling. In front of us, stretching far into the distance was a seemingly never ending corridor lined with translucent shimmering curtains of light, each of a different colour and similar to the one we had entered this place by. Shooting to and fro across this limitless space were countless wisps of light heading in all directions.

I looked behind me to question Zull but he had vanished, and to my astonishment, the portal, through which we had just passed, was no longer there. It was replaced by a continuation of that same corridor disappearing into oblivion in the opposite direction.

Not knowing what to do or where to go, we stood there watching those endless streams of light streaking back and forth. Then suddenly, and seemingly out of thin air, a figure appeared in front of us. I couldn't believe what I was seeing at first. He was dressed in a smart grey suit with a tie to match. He had immaculately coiffured grey white hair which was neatly slicked back, and a pair of highly polished black shoes adorned his feet. Apart from a halo of white light which surrounded him, he appeared to be a normal human being, which considering the paranormal events we had been bombarded with, made us think we would never see anything normal again. There was silence between us for a couple of minutes. I was thinking, and I guess we were all thinking, he may not be real and would disappear in a puff of smoke any minute. He was real enough though, probably the only real thing we had come across throughout the whole experience.

He didn't speak; he just pointed to a green shimmering curtain of light in that endless corridor in front of us and bade us to enter. Oddly enough none of us seemed to think twice about it, realising of course we now had no option. We had made our choice so there was no turning back, it just seemed the right thing to do. We stepped into the curtain, or should I say floated through it, and found ourselves surrounded by a very light and pleasant green mist. Again there were no walls or ceiling to be seen, and as outside, there were more of those wisps of light flashing to and fro in every direction.

Jason asked what those things were dashing about all over the place. The answer was bizarre

"Spirits," was the short answer.

"Spirits?" repeated Rod. "What spirits?"

"Human spirits," he answered. "Just like you are now, take a look."

We all turned and looked at each other. To our horror our bodies had disappeared. I remember Jason screaming out loud.

"Don't panic," said the man. "It is only a temporary thing until you have completed the process."

"What process?" asked Bill. "And what is this place?"

The man grinned and held up his hand to stop the flow of questions. "I will answer any questions you have, but first let me introduce myself. You will know me as the operator. I will be here to guide you and help you in any way I can." He indicated all around him. "I am in charge of this sector, which is one of many we operate here. You have no doubt noticed the many different coloured portals, which are doorways to these sectors and each one is assigned to a particular life form." He sensed we were totally out of our depth and unable to grasp what he was trying to tell us. "Let me explain," he continued. "We have a sector which deals with the bird species. We have another sector which deals with all aquatic life and another sector for insects and so on. As you have realised by now, this one deals with human life forms, which is why you are here as my guests."

Rod was puzzled by the term guest. The operator answered by saying we had entered here of our own free will and he was here to help us and guide us with whatever path we chose to go down. In the end it was up to each of us to decide our future.

"What happened to the world?" cried Jason. "Where is everybody?"

"Nothing has happened to the world," replied the operator. "It is carrying on as normal."

"But there's nobody out there."

"Oh but there is. You just couldn't see them, and they couldn't see you because I put you in a parallel time slot. You found yourself in an earlier time slot because it was the only one available, but it didn't really matter which one you were in."

"So you were controlling us all the time," remarked Bill.

The operator smiled and nodded. "Yes up to a point I was."

"I have a feeling," I said. "You could have brought us straight here, and yet you chose to put us through that ordeal, why?"

"Yes I could have brought you straight here. I make no apologies for not doing so. You were deliberately put in that stressful situation to make you realise how much better you coped with a situation like that when you all pull together. Each one of you has a strong point and a weak point. I put you in that situation to see how you would interact with each other."

"What was the point of that time bubble?" asked Rod. "You nearly lost us there."

"Yes, I must admit that incident was unfortunate. It is very rare for one of those to attach itself to another time zone. I did cut out the engine of your vehicle when I saw you heading towards the time warp, but unfortunately, you Jason, took it on yourself to enter the bubble. I did try to keep the zone there for as long as I could, but we have limited control over them. I am pleased to say that with Rod's limited knowledge you managed to escape it, which proves my point about all pulling together."

"Why have we been brought here, and what is all this talk about paths to take?"

He looked at each of us in turn for a moment. "I mean no offence by what I have to tell you. It is vital you listen very carefully to me and accept what I have to say, otherwise you cannot be helped. All creatures when they start a new life have a number of flaws. In the case of human beings, some have minor ones such as being obstinate or subject to temper tantrums, and many overcome these as they progress. Some develop nasty ones such as an uncaring nature or greed or aggressiveness or worse. Some realise they have become this way and are successful in ridding themselves of these terrible flaws, but there are those who are only too ready to exploit their flaws. There is nothing we can do for them and they will deserve their fate. Then there are others who do not realise they are this way. They are unaware of the detrimental effect they have on other people, especially their loved ones. That is where we can help, but only if they are willing."

"You are talking about us, aren't you?" said Rod.

"Yes," replied the operator. We all looked at each other. "I know what you are all thinking," he said. "You are saying to yourselves there is nothing wrong with me, why am I here?"

"Well I'm not aggressive or greedy," cried Jason.

"It doesn't have to be any of the ones I have pointed out, Jason. It is some point in your life where a different decision was called for."

"What?" said Jason. "What decision are you talking about?"

The operator shook his head. "I'm afraid I can't tell you. This is what the process is about."

"Tell us about this process," said Bill.

"Each one of you," answered the operator. "Will be sent back through your life, where hopefully each of you will recognise that point where a critical decision was needed to change the dangerous path each of you is treading."

"Dangerous path? I said. "What dangerous path?"

"With your permission, I am going to show each of you how your life will be if you continue as you are. Are you willing to do that?"

He gazed at each of us in turn, and then turned to Jason. "Don't be afraid. There is nothing to be frightened of. You are simply going to relive part of your life over again."

"But that's going to take years," cried Jason.

The operator grinned. "It will seem like years, but in fact no time will have elapsed from the moment you go to the moment you return."

"How is that possible?" fired back Jason.

"Don't worry your head about it," he replied. "Let's just say we have the ability to adjust time. All I need to know now is, are you gentlemen ready to take this first step?"

"We all made our choice before we entered the outer portal," said Rod. "I think I speak for everybody when I say we can't turn back now."

"What if I don't want to do this?" Jason suddenly blurted out.

"If any of you decide not to go through the process, I will send you back to the point where I intervened. That is the point at which I opened the portal to Hays Heath mine.

"So it was you who put that air door there?" cried Bill.

"Yes of course, but this time it will not be there, and you will carry on as you would have done and your memory of any of this will be erased. Before you make that decision, however, I would urge you to let me show you where your life is leading. If after you have seen it and you still do not want to continue, you will be returned as promised. Or you can become one of those." He pointed towards the wisps of light darting in all directions across the inky blackness above us.

"You must be joking," growled Jason. "Flying pointlessly across the sky forever. I don't think so."

"Oh they are not pointless," came back the operator. "They gather very useful information. They are vital to our work. They gathered information about you for instance."

"Can't we just go back through that door?" pleaded Jason.

I had to step in at this point. "You speak for yourself, Jason. I don't want to go back out there and neither do Bill and Rod. If you want to go back out there you go alone, but think very carefully about it. You will be going back to a world where you would be the only person in it? You would be condemning yourself to wander a desolate planet for eternity with no one to talk to or listen to. I don't think that is a prospect to look forward to, is it? Now you have a chance to go back and put your life back on the right track."

"But...but." spluttered Jason.

"Don't tell me that you haven't made any life changing mistakes," I said. "Because you clearly have or you wouldn't be here."

He looked at the operator, his face drained of colour. "I suppose you are right," he said, shrugging his shoulders. "Ok, I'm ready to take the chance."

It was at this point that Greg brought the story to a halt and stood to his feet "That's as far as I can go for now," he said. "The lads will be telling you their own stories from this point, Peter. Now I suspect you may be hungry, and I'm sorry, I don't have any food in the house to offer you, but if you want to go home and grab a bite to eat, I wondered if I could impose on you to come back after your meal and listen to the rest of the story? It's up to you of course, I wouldn't blame you if you felt it all boring and irrelevant, but I can't tell you how important it is for us for you to hear what we have to tell you."

"Yes of course," I replied. "In fact I'm quite intrigued. I will go and grab a bite to eat. I shall be back at say 2 o'clock."

12

I was back at Harley House at 2pm sharp. I was genuinely intrigued by where this story was leading and why they were all so anxious for me to hear it. After all, what I had heard up till now from Greg and Jason was about the dark side of their life. If that was me I wouldn't have wanted a stranger to know about my failings, but here they were insisting I hear it. I must admit I was bursting to tell someone, but I had promised I would not breathe a word of this to anyone, and it was a promise I intended to keep.

All was quiet as I reached the house. The rusting gate gave its usual high pitched squeal as I pushed it open, and closed it. I walked slowly up the uneven crazy paved path to the rear door, slowing down as I tried to peer through the grimy kitchen windows. It was deathly quiet, and I did wonder if they were all grabbing some sleep. I hesitated to knock on the door in case I disturbed them, and thought perhaps I should give them another hour. However, I found the kitchen door open slightly, and as I was about to push it open to peer inside it was suddenly pulled wide, and was greeted by Greg with a grin on his face. He ushered me to the living room, telling me to make myself comfortable. "I'm glad you came back," he said, as he entered the room. "I wouldn't have blamed you if you hadn't," he chuckled. "It is a bit much to take in."

"Not at all," I replied "It's an unusual story, I grant you that, but I am genuinely interested in where all this is leading."

Greg settled back in his easy chair. "Now, I will take you a little further, and then one of the others will tell you his side of the story." He looked at the others. "If you remember I took Peter up to the point where the operator wanted to show us how our lives would have been had we continued as we were, and we had reached the point where we had decided to take part in the process. Does anybody want to add anything before we begin?" They looked at each other in turn, but remained silent. "Ok," said Greg "let's begin. The operator chose Jason to be the first. I sensed he knew what was running through Jason's head and had selected him before he had a chance to change his mind. Now take it from here, Jason."

Jason ran his fingers through his thick mass of blonde hair and scratched at the back of his head. "I had no doubt that Greg's intuition about the operator was correct. My heart was pounding. I was scared out of my mind wondering what was going to happen. I was entering the unknown and I would be alone, and would no longer have the lads there to give me advice and encouragement, but the operator gave me no chance to change my mind. He quickly led me through that shimmering curtain of light to a long row of tubular transparent cubicles. He pointed to one of them and ushered me inside. The doors slid shut and the cubicle filled with a swirling mist. Within seconds the mist cleared and I could see I had been taken back to my childhood. I was sitting on a well-worn sofa listening to my mother lambasting my father. I was unashamedly enjoying it, because it was another argument I had deliberately caused. I suppose I had always been a difficult child. A bad tempered sullen little brat who would sulk for days if I didn't get my own way, and this was the main reason I didn't get on with my father, because he refused to give way to my unreasonable demands like my mother did, but she only gave way for peace and quiet and I knew this and played on it. My father on the other hand, was astute enough to know that giving in to my demands as a child would have repercussions in later life. He never gave up trying to win me round, but I constantly rejected him. As I have said, I was just an evil little brat persistently playing my parents against each other, and always to the detriment of my father. I probably didn't realise I was doing it at first, but as I grew older, I began to use it to my advantage. This, as you can imagine, caused an enormous amount of arguments between my parents. It became a vicious spiral, until my father, unable to bear the atmosphere in the house, took to going out most nights and coming back home worse for wear. Mother suffered this for a few years, but like my father, she was unable to cope anymore with the situation and walked out on us, leaving my father and me to fend for ourselves. We never heard from her again and we never found out where she had gone. She seemed to vanish off the face of the earth. It never occurred to me at the time that I was the cause of all this misery, I was too busy being a little monster to realise what I was doing to my parents.

This situation had worked the wrong way round as far as I was concerned. If it had been my father who had walked out, I wouldn't have batted an eyelid; in fact I would have been delighted. It would have left me to wrap my mother round my little finger.

My father sank deeper into his drink befuddled world and became incapable of looking after me. For the most part we ignored each other. We were just ships that passed in the night, leaving me to fend for myself.

Instead of going to school, I wandered the streets making a nuisance of myself. I was given every opportunity to make things better for myself, but I wouldn't listen. I didn't want to conform to any rules. Why would I want to be tied down by rules? They were for idiots. I was a free person, free to do as I pleased and nobody was going to tell me what to do.

That was all about to end though. Just after my fourteenth birthday, my father departed this Earth. In a drunken stupor he had stumbled across the road into the path of a lorry. He was rushed to hospital, but was so seriously injured he died in the ambulance on the way. You know what? I didn't care, in fact I am ashamed to say, I felt relieved. I didn't shed one single tear. As far as I was concerned he had become a stranger. I didn't even go to the funeral. Whether my mother went, I don't know. If she did she never made any effort to contact me, and who could have blamed her?

As a result of my father's death I was now considered an orphan, and being a notoriously difficult child, nobody was willing to take me in. Consequently I was taken into care, and as you can imagine I hated every minute of it. I was constantly in trouble, stealing drink and cigarettes from anywhere I could break into. It was impossible for anyone to control me, and eventually I ended up in a young offender's institution which had the effect of sending me on even more of a downward spiral. Drink and drugs were rife in there and the authorities seemed helpless to stop it. I knew I was out of control, and gradually came to realise that if I didn't make an effort I would end up killing myself.

I had always had a penchant for anything electrical, which the authorities fortunately recognised. I was offered a training programme while I was in the institution, and in one of my rare moments of wisdom; I decided this course might help put me back on the straight and narrow once I got released. I did well on my course surprisingly enough, and I'll give the authorities their due, they persuaded Blacks Engineering to give me a trial period on my release. I should have been grateful that someone, knowing my background, had shown some faith in me. It was good at first. I had a job to go to each day. I was learning a trade, and the management did their best to help me."

Jason fell quiet for a moment and glanced at each of us in turn. "You can feel there's a but coming on, can't you? The problem was," he continued. "The money was barely a living wage and I was living in a poky one bedroom council flat in a rundown area. I wanted better than that. I wanted money in my pockets and I knew where to get it. In a fit of depression one night I contacted one of the lads from the institution who I had been close to while I was in there. It was a bad mistake; in fact it was more than that, it was a disaster. I should have left well alone, I know that now.

I got involved in drug dealing. I made a lot of money, but the more I made the more I spent on my drug addiction and drinking. I was again spiralling out of control. I began taking time off from work. There were mornings I just couldn't get out of bed, and when I did turn in for work I couldn't concentrate. The management frequently hauled me into the office, at first accepting my excuses, then warning I must do better or I would be dismissed. Rod took me under his wing. We talked for hours on end about my problem. He told me more than once he could see the potential in me, and if I could get a grip on myself I would make a first class electrician. It was great to have someone like him have a bit of faith in you, seemingly more than I had in myself. I did try, but I was weak willed. I just wasn't strong enough to overcome the pull of the drugs.

Then on that Thursday night before the Easter weekend, Rod called at my flat to tell me he wanted me along with him on an emergency call out at the Sandford Valley mine. I protested that it was the Easter weekend and I was looking forward to having a drink with my friends. He explained, that providing there were no problems they would be able to complete the inspection in one day. There would be an extra day tagged on so we would still get the four days, plus there was double pay. To any right minded person this was not to be missed, but all I could think of was my weekend with my friends at the Black Star public house.

I made all sorts of excuses not to go, but he wouldn't leave until I promised I would be at work no later than eight the next morning. I closed the door and stood for a moment thinking about the double pay, it would certainly have come in useful. I returned to my living room and sat myself down. I remember thinking that Rod was a good friend and was trying to help me get back on my feet, but then the pull of a few drinks with the old gang proved to be too strong, and before I knew it I was making my way to the Black Star public house.

The Black Star was a place where no self-respecting person would enter. It was a place I used to frequent a lot, and it mattered not I was under age. It used to be regularly raided by the drug squads, but they gave that up long ago. The attitude of the police nowadays was that it kept the druggies and wino's off the streets, and they knew where to find them if they wanted them. Needless to say I never made it to work the next day, in fact I never even made it back to my flat. I woke up freezing cold the next morning on a park bench.

I stumbled into work after Easter only to be informed my services were no longer required. From that moment on my life took a nosedive. I was unable to pay my rent because I was spending my money on drink and drugs and I ended up being thrown out of my flat. I was reduced to a life walking the streets and dossing down wherever I could.

The operator now moved me on. I found myself standing outside a dilapidated five story building, which I recognised as Greston's woollen mill. The once thriving red brick Victorian building was now abandoned and derelict. Most of its metal window frames had rusted and fallen out. The ones which had managed to remain in place had most of the dirt ingrained panes smashed out by the hordes of kids who used the building as a playground. The once impressive main doors hung drunkenly from their hinges where intruders had forced their way in looking for anything that was saleable. The huge loading bays, which once echoed to the sound of trucks being loaded with goods, now lay as silent as a graveyard and littered with untidy mounds of wood and rubble and bits of rusting machinery, giving a home to a plethora of weeds and insects. Shrubs had pushed themselves up through the widening cracks in the great expanse of the concrete surface.

I found myself warily entering a gloomy foul smelling room, whose windows were so grimed they allowed in only the minimum of light. Rat and bird droppings covered almost the entire concrete floor which was dotted with small craters where machinery had been unceremoniously ripped out of their beds. Enormous cobwebs hung like grey curtains from every light fitting and corner.

My eyes came to rest on a mound of disintegrating stained blankets heaped on an equally stained and torn mattress in a corner of the room. Suddenly the air was filled with the sound of sirens, and moments later the room was crisscrossed with torch beams as the police entered the room. A young lad, who had accompanied the police, pointed to the pile of blankets. As several beams concentrated on them, the attending doctor approached and peeled back the blankets. It revealed an unconscious figure. I recoiled in horror as I stared into those bloodshot eyes and recognised the gaunt, yellow wrinkled face, as mine.

"He's still alive, just," announced the doctor, indicating to the waiting ambulance men to whisk me off to hospital. In an instant the scene faded and I found myself in a room full of medical equipment, where a doctor was administering shock treatment to my lifeless body. I watched as my body arched several times as he applied the treatment. Finally he switched off the machine and shook his head. "He's gone I'm afraid. There is nothing more we can do for him. Do we know who he is? Does he have any family?"

The ward sister shook her head. "Apparently he is an alcoholic drug addict with no friends or family. According to the police," commented the sister. "They have moved him on from place to place for years."

"Why people do this to themselves I will never know," sighed the doctor. "By the sound of it, dying is the best thing that could have happened to him." He then held up the sheet ready to cover my face. "Well son," he said staring down at me. "The next move will be your last. You are off to the mortuary now where we have a nice cardboard coffin waiting for you."

I was in shock. I couldn't believe what I had just seen. I stared open mouthed at the operator. "I don't really end up like that, do I?"

He gave me a steely gaze. "That is your destiny if you continue as you are."

"But I did turn up for work," I said. "I didn't go to the Black Star."

"That was through my intervention," he said. "I am showing you the path you were on. This is the path you will stay on if you do not wish to partake in the process and wish to return. Before you say anything let me show you more."

Once again the mist descended and then slowly cleared. I found myself looking down on a large modern detached house set in a beautifully kept garden. Three young children were splashing happily in a portable paddling pool. I could see myself on the patio of the house keeping a close eye on them. A beautiful young lady, who I took to be my wife, was by my side. We were holding hands and laughing and were obviously very happy. The scene then faded and I found myself being helped from the cubicle by the operator.

"That," he said. "Is the kind of life you could have if you are willing to take part in the process. If you do not, and still want to return to your old life, just say the word and I will return you."

"No, no," I yelled. "I will do it. Let's get started."

"Not just yet. I have to have answers from the others first."

He led me to a large luxuriously furnished brightly lit room. The furnishings were as I have never seen before, but very comfortable. The walls seemed to be translucent and emanating soft multi-coloured light. A soothing sound was being played but it wasn't music as we know it.

"Make yourself comfortable in here," he said. "I will be back to you shortly."

13

"The operator suddenly appeared before us," said Rod. "He didn't say anything, he just pointed to me and beckoned for me to enter that curtain of green light." Rod then turned to Greg. "Shall I continue with my story?"

Greg nodded. "Please carry on."

"I was confronted by a row of transparent cubicles," continued Rod. "The operator informed me he would be taking me back through my life. This time, he said he was going to show me how it would be if I carried on the way I was doing and not to be frightened because my own fate was in my own hands. That statement alone filled me with dread. According to him, it seems none of us were making a very good job of our lives, so to say that my own fate rested in my own hands was most unnerving. How can you not be frightened when you don't know what to expect. Anyway, I didn't have time to think about it before I was fastened in one of the cubicles and was taken back to my youth."

Rod stretched out his long legs and clasped his hands to the back of his head. "I suppose I was a typical young lad, you know, brash and full of life, knowing it all and chasing women. Though it was not my behaviour to women which gave me a bad reputation. Let me explain.

My parents weren't exactly poor, but neither could they afford the little luxuries in life. My father had at one time worked in the coal mines, which in those days it was poorly paid work. Eventually he had to leave because of the dust getting on his chest and took a job as a night watchman. The pay was even worse, but at least he wasn't breathing in that choking coal dust. My mother took a part time job as a till operator at the local supermarket to bring in a little extra, but even then my parents had to count every penny. However, they had brought me up to be a well-mannered and honest citizen, and up until leaving school I lived up their expectations. Without sounding too swelled headed, I had a good brain on me and I had studied hard at school, but by the time I had come to leave, a recession was sweeping the country and jobs were few and far between. Long before leaving school I had made my mind up I wanted to be an electrician. I was always playing about with all sorts of electrical appliances, stripping them down to see how they worked and then trying to put them back together.

I trudged the streets for weeks looking for work, but it was hopeless. The kind of work I had set my heart on was just not available. I felt that all that stuff my parents had drummed into me about studying hard at school would pay me dividends when I left, had been a complete waste of time. I had worked hard at school, and for what? To end up walking the streets looking for work that just wasn't there. I would have loved to go to college, but there was no way my parents could afford it. That's when I fell into a life of crime. It's a fact that hanging around street corners bored out your mind with a like-minded bunch of lads, is a recipe for trouble.

It had started with four of us breaking into a shop. With a young mans testosterone coming to the fore, and with each of us trying to show the others how brave we were. It was no more than devilment brought on by sheer boredom. It was a fruit shop of all places, which was how much brains we had between us. There was nothing in the till as anyone with any intelligence would have known. No business ever left money in the till, but being the raw amateurs we were, we didn't know that. We just messed up the shop in frustration, but seeing it reported in the newspaper the next day gave us all a thrill. We decided to break into another shop, this time we picked on a newsagent. Our thinking was, if the till was empty, at least we could steal the cigarettes and stuff ourselves with chocolate. We got caught this time though trying to sell the cigarettes we had stolen. Luckily, because we were so young and it was a first offence we were all let off with a warning. Mum and Dad were horrified, and although our names didn't get into the newspaper, it didn't take long for word to spread. Mum and Dad said they were too ashamed to go out and restricted me to the house at night, but gave way to my pleas to look for a job in the daytime. Unfortunately the time of day doesn't stop you getting into trouble. I was actually out looking for work when I stumbled across Jack, one of the lads I had broken into the newsagents with.

"What are you up to?" he asked.

"Looking for work," I replied.

"Mug's game," he growled, pulling out a wad of money and waving it under my nose. "Look at that. When was the last time you saw that much money?" he sneered.

I remember staring at it wide eyed. "Where did you get that from?" I gasped.

He stuffed it quickly back in his pocket. "Didn't have to beg and scrape to some toffee nosed boss, did I? And there's plenty more where that came from. I'm going to get myself a motorbike next week. I bet you would like a motor bike eh?"

"I sure would," I sighed.

"Then come and join us and earn yourself some money."

"Doing what?" I asked.

I remember he looked at me as though I was stupid. "What do you think?" he grunted.

"Not robbery?" I exclaimed. "What if we get caught again? It will be prison next time."

He screwed up his face. "We were a bit green last time. We only got caught because we were trying to sell those cigarettes on the street. This time we don't have to go around the streets trying to sell it. We take anything we get to somebody who buys it all from us. It's money for nothing. I've done dozens of jobs since then; it's like taking candy from a kid."

I hesitated. "I err... I don't know." I said. I must admit though, I was envious of Jack with his pocket full of money.

He grinned and patted his bulging pocket. "You'd like some of this wouldn't you?"

I nodded meekly. "Yes, but I err..."

"Have a think about it," he grunted. He pointed to a café across the street. "If you want in, I shall be in there on Wednesday morning." He made off across the street.

For two days I turned it over and over in my mind. That wad of notes Jack had waved under my nose kept popping into my head, it was just what I needed to put me through college, but I was scared of getting caught and it would almost certainly finish off my parents.

It had now reached Wednesday morning and I was still wrestling with the decision. It should have been an easy one to make and it should have been no, but I was too weak willed to say no to the money. The thought of going to college was too tempting and I could see no other way of affording it. I lied to my parents, telling them I had found work at some non-existent factory miles away and they would loan me the money to go to college. My parents were delighted of course, both of them praising me for my efforts to stay on the straight and narrow."

There was a long pause from Rod. He gave a deep sigh. There were signs of tears welling up in his eyes. He wiped them away with the back of his hand. He took a long intake of breath to stem the tears and continued.

"I know I should have felt terribly guilty about my lies to them, but I didn't. In fact I didn't have a conscious about it at all. As far as I was concerned I wasn't hurting anyone and the money was going to be put to good use. I did several jobs with the boys, all small time robberies, and the more I did the more confident I got. That was until someone decided we should go for something bigger, and planned a raid on a factory safe. I wasn't happy, I wasn't happy at all, but as a member of the gang I had to go along with it.

The scene changed to where I was the lookout posted in a telephone box a few yards up the road from the factory gates. If I saw anyone approach the factory I was to telephone a warning to the main office where someone would be waiting. Suddenly the air was filled with sirens as a trio of police cars came racing towards the factory. It turned out someone hadn't done their homework properly and had set off an alarm which only rang at the police station. I rang the number as soon as I saw the police racing to the scene, and made my escape, as did the getaway driver. They were all caught with the exception of myself. I was shocked to read in the newspaper they had roughed up the night watchman to such an extent, that the poor man, because of his injuries, may be unable to work again. I thought of dad at this point. He was a night watchman, it could have been him, but I consoled myself it wasn't, so it didn't matter did it? They were all sent to prison for varying terms. I gave the lads their due, they never grassed me up. I uprooted myself quickly before the police came sniffing round to my house. I told my parents I was going to a college in the North. I didn't want them to know I had headed here to Garton in case the police did go round there. I chose Garton because I knew there was a pretty good engineering college here and enrolled for the course.

After college I got myself a good job at Black's engineering, where I met Dawn. I thought she was the most beautiful girl I had ever met. She had long flowing shiny blonde hair and the most penetrating deep blue eyes I had ever seen. What I fell for was her bubbly nature and lovely sense of humour. She had a little turned up nose which twitched when she laughed. It was instant bonding for both of us and we became inseparable. We went everywhere and did everything together, but whenever she asked about my past I would trundle out a few white lies, telling her I took odd jobs here and there to get my money to go to college. She did suggest a couple of times about meeting my parents, but I put her off by telling her they were in a home and too frail for visitors. I never wanted to visit my hometown again in case I bumped into any of the gang.

Dawn and I were good together. We had planned to get married as soon as we left college, but I was always frightened my past would catch up with me, and one day it did.

The operator whisked me forward to late one afternoon. I was leaving the factory in a hurry to get home to Dawn, so I didn't take too much notice of the figure lurking by the main gate. As I walked past him he called out.

"Not speaking, Rod?"

I stood stock still for a moment. The voice was familiar. I whirled round to face him. My heart sank when I saw it was Jack.

"You haven't forgotten your old friend, have you Rod?"

My stomach churned and I felt the colour drain from my face. I was in a state of shock but I had to play this cool. "Hello Jack," I said, doing my best to put on my brightest smile. "What brings you to this part of the world?"

"I was just passing through and thought I would look you up to see how you are."

If you knew Jack like I did, you just knew he was lying and was up to something. I didn't want him following me home and meeting Dawn. I didn't want him telling her about my criminal past. I suggested we go for a beer so we could chat about old times. We made our way to the nearest bar and settled into a secluded corner out of earshot. I banged a couple of pints down on the table.

"What the heck are you doing here, Jack?" I spat. "How on earth hell did you find me?"

"Now then Rod, that's no way to greet an old pal, is it?"

"We're not pals," I growled. "We never were. We did a few jobs together that was all. I've moved on now, I've put the past behind me."

Jack took a good swallow of his beer. "Easy for you, isn't it Rod? Not so easy for me and the lads though is it with prison records hanging round our necks? Police banging on my door every time there's a robbery in the area." Jack leaned forward and gave me a menacing stare. "Now listen to me Rod my boy," he hissed "You haven't got a police record because we didn't grass you up. We think you owe us big time for that."

My heart sank. I knew what was coming. "I'm not doing any more jobs, Jack?"

"That's not very friendly, is it, Rod? Considering the lads kept you out of prison. I don't suppose for one minute you have told your wife what you've been up to."

I glared at him for a minute. "And what makes you think I'm married?"

"It's Dawn, isn't it?" he grinned. "I even know where you live. I know all about your cosy little life here, Rod."

My stomach turned. "You just keep away from her," I growled.

He gave a sarcastic little grin. "Don't worry. I won't have to if you are a good lad." He held up his empty glass. "Time for another I think."

I snatched the glass from his grasp and marched to the bar. "My heart was beating like a jungle drum. I had to do something, but what? I hurried back to the table with the drinks. "Now look here, Jack," I hissed. If you go anywhere near her…"

"It's no good threatening me, Greg. I won't breathe a word, but I can't speak for the rest of the lads."

I knew it was no good arguing with him. It wasn't Jack I should be frightened of. It was the rest of the lads. I knew them well enough to know they would carry out their threats. Even if Dawn stood by me, it would be the end of my parents.

"What do you want, Jack?" I growled.

"We want your help with a job."

"No!" I could hear myself shouting. I could sense the bar had gone quiet and all eyes were focused on our table.

"I'd calm myself down if I were you," grunted Jack. "You don't want the whole world knowing your business, do you?"

"No Jack," I hissed. "I've told you I'm finished with that game."

"I don't think so," he sneered. "You've got a history, Rod. It will always be there. You can't get away from it. It's already caught up, with you, and it will again. You might as well make some money from it while you can."

"You mean you lot will keep coming back to haunt me. I just want to be left alone, Jack. Is that too much to ask?"

"Do this one job and I'll persuade the boys to leave you alone. It's big money, there will be enough in your share to buy you a nice house and whatever you want for it. Won't your missus love that?"

"It's tainted money" I growled. "I don't want it."

"It was good enough in the old days, wasn't it Rod? It didn't matter then it was tainted did it? I dare say it helped put you through college."

I couldn't answer him because I knew he was right. My past would always be there to haunt me. These guys were never going to let go. If I didn't do what they wanted they would see to it I would never hold down a decent job again. I couldn't see any way out of the situation. I had to think quickly. "Sounds very tempting," I said, trying to sound interested. "Give me a few days to think about it."

"I need to know by Tuesday. The job is on Wednesday."

"That's coming up to Easter weekend."

"That's right. That's when the safes are full of money ready for the Easter break payout."

I felt sick to my stomach. Just as I had put all that bad stuff behind me and was enjoying life with a wonderful woman, up pops Jack like a bad smell threatening to ruin it all. I felt I had no choice but to go along with it. I promised to meet him in the Rose and Crown on Tuesday night.

My mind wasn't on my work that Tuesday. I seemed to spend the day in a twilight zone. I was angry. Angry that Jack was threatening to rake up my shameful past deeds. I hardly spoke a word on the way home that night. I played with my meal shoving it from one side of the plate to the other. Dawn asked if I was ok. I tried to pretend I was, but she saw right through me. She knew something was troubling me when I asked if she minded if I went out for a drink, but being the diplomat she was, she never questioned me anymore.

I entered the bar at the Rose and Crown later that evening, hoping against hope that Jack would not be there. It was not to be though, as I walked into the room, there he was as large as life at a table as near to the door as he could get. It was obvious he had been in the Rose and Crown for quite a while by the amount of cigarette butts in the ashtray. The one thing I remembered about Jack was the number of cigarettes he smoked, and the amount of whisky he could put away without having the slightest effect on him.

"I don't want to talk here," I said. "There are too many ears listening to us. I know somewhere quiet where we can discuss this." I led him along a narrow dirt track road through a wooded area to a stone built bridge that crossed over a now disused railway track.

"I knew you would turn up," grinned Jack. "The money was too much of a temptation, wasn't it?"

I could have knocked that silly grin off his face. "If you really want to know, I nearly didn't turn up, I snarled."

"Don't give me that," He grunted. He whipped a huge bundle of money from his pocket and wafted it in front of my face. "You thought about this, didn't you? What's that saying, Rod, once a thief always a thief?"

I suddenly saw red at that remark. I snatched the bundle of notes from his hand and threw it over the parapet. "You can keep your money," I yelled at him. He rushed to the parapet and leaned over to see his money land on the track below. In a moment of temper I picked up a rock and rammed it as hard as I could into the back of his head. He gave a groan and his body slumped limply across the parapet. I was frozen to the spot. I stood horrified for a moment at the thought of what I had done. I tried in vain to bring him round before realising to my horror, he was dead. I was now panicking and I felt my stomach doing somersaults. I rushed into the undergrowth to be violently sick. My first thought was to get out of there as fast as I could, but I thought better of it. I had to cover my tracks. Gathering my thoughts, I heaved his body up and over the parapet and listened as his body hit the ground below with a sickening thud. My theory was, that because I knew Jack had consumed a fair amount of alcohol, they would think he had fallen over in a drunken stupor. I slung the rock as far as I could into the bushes and made my way to the Rose and Crown. I had the presence of mind to think about cleaning my shoes before I went home to get rid of any evidence of me ever being along that lane. Luckily there was no blood on my clothes and Dawn had gone to bed.

The police weren't fooled though, and it wasn't long before they had established that Jack was a known criminal and were working on the theory it was a gangland murder. They were, however, unable to find out what he was doing in the area. It may have seemed I had got away with it, but they never give up do they. Now I froze every time there was a knock on the door. My heart thumped like a hammer against my chest every time the phone rang. There were times I wanted to run into the police station and scream IT WAS ME! IT WAS ME! But the consequences of a life in prison stopped me. I was having sleepless nights with the strain of not having the guts to confess all to Dawn.

At that point the operator appeared. "Please tell me this isn't my future," I pleaded. "This is not the person I am."

"You mean this is not the person you *want* to be," he answered. "Unfortunately, because you thought only of yourself, this is the person you have become. You made decisions to suit only yourself regardless of how they affected others, and consequently you made dangerous errors of judgements along the way. Let me show you more."

"The operator took me to the night that Greg had phoned me. My mind was in a state of turmoil, I couldn't think straight. I knew that once the gang found out about what had happened to Jack, they would put two and two together and would come calling. They didn't know where I lived, but it would only be a matter of time before they did. Dawn would ditch me. She wasn't going to be married to a criminal and I had already told her lies. I thought about once again uprooting myself and starting a new life in some other town, but sooner or later they would find me, and it would start all over again. This poor girl had enough on her plate at the moment without me adding to it. She was suffering from a mystery illness which was causing her a lot of pain in her hands and legs and was now undergoing tests to determine what the cause of it was

Dawn and I had planned to take our little caravan down to the coast during the Easter break, but I wasn't really looking forward to it with all that on my mind. Dawn was quite astute when it came to guessing what mood I was in, and would have known there was something amiss. The last thing I wanted was a barrage of questions right now, so when Greg phoned me on that Thursday night, telling me I was needed for the mine inspection, the timing couldn't have been better. It would give me time to think things out, although I didn't want to sound too pleased about it.

After we spoke, I put the phone down and prepared to give Dawn the news. I made my way to the kitchen where she was preparing a meal. I was trying to look disappointed as I informed her it was Greg who had phoned. She immediately thought it was to do with Sylvia. Even when I told it was to do with work she didn't cotton on it involved me. She just expressed surprise that Greg was going into work at Easter.

Dawn did have a tendency to chatter on. I had to interrupt the flow of words "I have to go with him." She stopped what she was doing and turned to face me. Her eyes widened and her mouth dropped open. She gave me one of those looks that made me feel the biggest cad of all time. "I'm sorry," was all I could muster.

"I don't believe it" she cried. "This was to be a nice holiday before I went into hospital."

I pulled her to me, telling her not to get upset. "It will only be a day's job," I said   trying to sound confident. "We'll soon have the inspection done. Greg is going to talk Harry into extending the holiday so we will still get our four day break. We can kick off on Saturday and not come back until Tuesday."

She stared at me for a moment. There was no emotion showing on her face. She wasn't angry but I could see a flicker of disappointment. "That's cutting it a bit fine isn't it?" she remarked in a matter of fact tone. "You know I have to be at the hospital Wednesday morning for more treatment." Suddenly there was a flood of tears. "I don't know why they are bothering. They are not getting any further with it. The treatment is not taking the pain away. Whatever they try makes no difference."

103

I was lost for words at first. She had never spoken like this before. She had always been upbeat about it. I suppose now the pain was getting to her. I hugged her tightly; cupping the back of her head in my hands. I looked directly into her eyes trying to say something positive. "Don't talk like that darling. You have got to have hope. They are constantly coming up with new treatments."

She tightened her grip on me. "I'm not frightened, Rod. They have told me there isn't much more they can do. I can accept that as long as you are here with me. That is why I was looking forward to this holiday so much."

"I told her not to worry. The job would only last a few hours and we would soon be on our way the next day. I'm a coward when it comes to illnesses, I just can't cope with it. So secretly I was glad I was going to get away from it for a while. I told myself she would be fine while I was away. It selfishly never crossed my mind she would be alone with her thoughts and wanted me by her side. She smiled at me and apologised for being so silly, and we were going to have a wonderful weekend. Feeling reassured she was now in a more settled frame of mind I went off to see Jason.

The scene changed. We had completed the inspection at the mine. I had dropped Jason off at his flat, warning him not to be late for work after the holidays. I arrived home to find the door wide open. I shouted Dawn's name as I entered the house. There was no reply. I shouted again and this time I heard a faint reply from the bedroom. I rushed up the stairs to see her stretched out on the bed fully dressed, her face bruised and drained of colour. She was too weak to move or answer any questions. I immediately phoned for an ambulance

In my next vision, I was in a private ward. I was sitting at the hospital bedside and Dawn had just come round. "What happened?" I asked. I had to put my ear close to her mouth to hear her reply. She told me two men had burst into the house shouting my name. "Who were they?" I asked. "They said they were friends of someone called Jack and they wanted some answers. Who is this Jack, Rod? What do they want?" I felt sick to my stomach. They had wasted no time in finding me. "Did they do this?" I said pointing to her bruised face. She didn't answer, she gave a moan and her eyes closed. The alarm sounded on the machine she was connected to, and suddenly the place was a hive of activity. I was ordered out of the room as nurses connected all sorts of tubes to her. After a while, I had no idea how long. The doctor switched off the alarm and everyone stood still. He strode to the door and sat beside me in the corridor. "I'm afraid we have lost her," he said. "If only you could have managed to get her to the hospital yesterday we might have had a chance." Those words were like a knife through my heart. Then I heard the operator's voice.

"It hasn't happened yet," he said. "But it will, unless you alter the course of your life. Let me show you how it can be."

A scene changed. Dawn and I were in a large hall. Music was playing in the background. We were happy and laughing and surrounded by people offering their congratulations. Apparently, I had some time ago started my own company which had now grown into a very successful business, and I had thrown this celebration for my employees to celebrate a record year.

"Wow, that is fantastic, "I gasped. "That looks good to me."

"As I have told you before," said the operator. "It hasn't happened yet. You have work to do to make it happen. Now let us return." In a flash He was showing me into a room exactly as Jason described. "I want you to relax here. I will be back soon."

14

"It was my turn next," said Bill. "And just like Rod, I didn't have a choice. The operator just led me through that curtain, and as we had not heard from Jason or Rod or knew what had happened to them, I was scared stiff at not knowing what to expect."

Bill eased himself back in his armchair and adjusted his cushion. "My story bears no relation to any of these guy's stories, except for Jason I suppose in a roundabout way. Unlike Jason though, it was my mother who I didn't get on with. In fact I hated her. She was a cruel, vain woman, who had no time for me and who treated my father like dirt.

The operator had taken me back to when I was a very unhappy thirteen year old child. I was living a miserable life in a grey terraced house in a warren of grey cobbled streets populated by grey people. This was Garton, and I felt as though I had been buried alive. Though now long gone, coal mining was the dominant industry, and with three coal mines all within close proximity of the town, it was far from the upmarket place you see today. Giant black slag heaps surrounded the town. Huge trucks piled high with coal thundered day and night through the towns narrow cobbled streets spilling their black dust everywhere, and permeating the ground and buildings wherever it came in contact with.

My father was one of those miners, toiling underground in the sweltering heat for a pittance, some weeks never seeing daylight. I have to say that times were hard then. In my house my father was the only one working, and the wage in the mining industry in those days was very poor, so there wasn't a lot of money coming into the house. My arrogant mother refused to work, saying it was his place to provide for his family and not expect his wife to demean herself by having to go out to work. She repeatedly needled him about our poor standard of living and how she struggled to make ends meet. That didn't stop her spending his hard earned money on a constant stream of clothes and shoes and cosmetics for herself, whilst my father and I had to make do with second hand items from the jumble sales. She never went through the door without dressing up and being plastered with make-up. On one rare occasion when my father did tackle her about it, she retaliated by saying he should be proud he had such a beautiful wife. I think there was no doubt in his mind she had another man tucked away somewhere. She would go out regularly in the evenings in all her finery, with the excuse she was meeting one of her lady friends and return home very late at night.

I did see her out with this man one night. She had left dad and me to get our own meals, which was a regular occurrence, while she went off to see her lover. Dad dug into his pocket one night and decided he was going to treat us both to some fish and chips. As I stood waiting my turn in the shop, she came strolling past the open door as bold as you like, holding hands with another man. I rushed home as soon as I had been served to tell my father.

"I've seen her Dad," I cried breathlessly.

"Calm down son," he said. "Seen who?"

My eyes filled with tears in a mixture of anger and sadness that this lovely man was being cheated on by my horrid mother. "My mother," I sobbed. "She was with another man. They were holding hands."

There was no reaction from him at all. Not a flicker of emotion crossed his face as he studied my sad tear filled eyes. He pulled me to him and hugged me tightly. "I know all about it, son. I have known for a good while. I think it serves the man right, don't you agree?"

I pulled away and looked at him. I never expected that reaction. I thought he would have been devastated, but he was smiling. Then with an ever widening grin, he said. "Let's keep our fingers crossed and hope she runs off with him. What do you say William?"

I burst out laughing, I couldn't help it, but at the same time I couldn't help feeling he was putting a brave face on it all. There were occasions when I would look at him and see he was aging before his time. There was a sadness in his eyes he couldn't hide. Why did he let this woman ride roughshod over him? I willed him to fight back, but he rarely did. I got the feeling as I grew older he thought arguing with her was a waste of breath, and he was   probably right, because she always had an answer for him.

I left school at the age of fifteen. Jobs were few and far between in those days but my father used his influence and got me a job at the mine where he worked. I settled into the job quite nicely, working on the surface until I was old enough to go underground.

The most prominent thing on a normal lad's mind at that age was girls. All my friends had girlfriends, if only for a month or two. It was natural behaviour, but I didn't subscribe to it. After experiencing what a woman had done to my father I wanted no part of it. It wasn't as though I couldn't get a girlfriend, in fact it was just the opposite. Although I say it myself I wasn't a bad looking lad and could have had numerous girlfriends, but I kept well away from them. My friends thought there was something wrong with me and I got teased quite a bit, but they could think what they wanted as far as I was concerned. When I heard their girlfriends getting on to them because they wanted to do something they didn't, I would smile and thank my lucky stars it wasn't me.

Up until I was about eighteen years of age, I had steadfastly refused to even date a girl, but then my hormones started to get the better of me. I decided there was nothing wrong in having the odd date or two. One night stands became the norm but I didn't want any commitments and the girls would have to understand that. Those that did try to get their claws into me were soon got rid of.

However, a few years down the line the inevitable happened. I met Wendy and I am still not sure to this day what happened, but she instantly captured my heart. What came over me I don't know, but that brick wall I had built between me and women suddenly crumbled. I was totally smitten with her. The feeling was alien to me and before I knew it I was asking her out on a date. To my surprise she said yes, and from there we went from strength to strength.

We eventually married, something I had sworn I would never do, but Wendy was like no other girl I had ever met. She was never demanding or extravagant, always careful to see we could afford the things we needed. She never objected if I wanted to go for a drink with my friends. She made it obvious she loved me very much by always putting my needs first. She was a far cry from that evil woman my father had married.

Looking back, Wendy was as near perfect as you could get. I say looking back, because I realise now, though not at the time, I still had issues relating to that torrid time my father had with my mother. Each time I thought Wendy was trying to tell me what to do, my mothers voice would echo around my head and I would react somewhat unnecessarily. This sort of behaviour obviously put a strain on the marriage. Wendy though was very understanding. I had explained what I had been through and she accepted the way I was. She was a wonderful woman, so why couldn't I see that at the time? And because I was allowed to get away with my bad attitude, I made no effort to do anything about it. One day it all came to a head.

My father for a long time had been suffering from more than the usual bouts of colds or flu. He refused to take time off work. For one thing, I don't think he wanted to spend any more time with my mother than necessary. For another, she would have nagged him constantly about losing pay, so to his detriment he would haul himself into work each day. Inevitably this took its toll on him and he became very ill, and was eventually confined to his bed. My mother selfishly refused to give up seeing her friends to stay at home and look after him. With the help of a kindly next door neighbour, we took care of him. He did eventually recover, but he was too weak to continue in the mines and had to rely on social security. That is when my mother put the boot in. That woman, that callous bitch, walked out on him, telling him he was a pathetic excuse of a man and useless to any woman and he couldn't expect her to live like a pauper. Had she said this to him a few years ago, he still would have been greatly upset but would have been strong enough to get over it. Why he loved this horrid woman I will never know. As it was, he was at his lowest ebb. If ever he needed her support it was now. He was distraught. How could she treat him like that? This man had worked all the hours possible to provide this egotistical uncaring woman with a roof over her head and this was his reward. When things had got tough, instead of standing by him she was off to live with her lover, leaving my father to fend for himself. I did offer for him to come and live with Wendy and me, but he was a proud man and wouldn't hear of it. I knew he wouldn't last long. That woman had destroyed his will to live, and he passed away a couple of months later.

Unfortunately, after the funeral, I began behaving like an idiot. Getting revenge on my mother had obsessed me. I began taking my anger for my mother out on Wendy. I spent hours trawling the streets trying to find her and her lover. I would come home from work and go straight out again. Wendy, needless to say, got very anxious about me. She thought I would make myself ill keeping up that pace all the time, and terrified of what I would do if I did manage to find her.

"Where will that leave me when you are in prison doing life?" she asked of me. "I beg you to forget this fixation of seeking revenge on your mother. She will get what she deserves believe me. What goes around comes around."

"I couldn't be pacified with this tired old cliché and never gave up the search. My mother wasn't going to get away with what she had done to my father. I vowed I would walk to the ends of the earth to reap justice.

On the Thursday before Easter, as I was about to finish work at the mine for the weekend, I was asked, as the safety officer, to escort Rod, Greg and Jason on an underground inspection. I wasn't too happy because I had planned to spend the weekend in search of my mother. I had only been home about thirty minutes when the phone rang. It was from a good friend of mine who worked at the travel agents to say he had found out my mother's address. Apparently, she and her man had called in to collect their holiday vouchers and her address was on the paperwork. I established they would be back after the Easter break.

I slammed down the phone. "I've found her," I snarled. "She is on holiday now but she is going to get what's coming to her when she gets back."

Wendy couldn't believe I was actually going through with it. She had thought all along my ranting and raving was all hot air and when it came to the crunch I would come to my senses. She was absolutely horrified to find I meant what I said. She threatened to leave me if I didn't stop this madness, but I was so consumed with hate I dismissed it as an idle threat. I took the lads on the inspection the next day, and I am ashamed to admit it, but my mind wasn't on my job. All I could think about was to confront my mother as soon as she got back.

The operator fast forwarded me to that Tuesday night. I couldn't believe what I was seeing. With a carving knife concealed under my long coat, I stepped into the night air with Wendy clinging to my arm. Once again she voiced her threat, but I ignored it and vanished into the night. The next thing I knew, I was hiding in the shadows of a dimly lit, deserted street. I hadn't had time to formulate a plan. If necessary I would have to kill both my mother and her new man.

As I watched, the door opened and my mother and a man I took to be her new boyfriend, appeared on the doorstep. He gave her a kiss and walked off down to the end of the street and turned a corner. She stepped back inside and closed the door. Without thinking, I marched up to the door and knocked. The door opened almost immediately, she must have thought her boyfriend had forgotten something. She was about to say something but the words froze on her lips. She stared at me for what seemed an eternity. "William!" she gasped. "What the heck are you doing here?"

I didn't answer. I whipped out the knife from under my coat. Before she had time to scream I plunged it into her chest with such force it almost reached the hilt. She fell back into the hall in a pool of blood. I quickly withdrew the knife and slammed the door shut and hastened away from the scene. I checked my clothes for blood stains, apart from my gloves which I disposed of, there were none. When I returned to the house, Wendy had gone. She had carried out her threat and had left. I never found where she had gone to, she seemed to have vanished off the face of the earth."

As Bill came to the part about stabbing his mother, I looked around at the others. None of them showed any emotion on their faces at the announcement that he had murdered his mother for what she had done to his father. It was as though it was an everyday occurrence. This made me feel distinctly uneasy. My brain was in turmoil. A lump came to my throat and I could feel the blood draining from my face. Had all four of them been involved in this plot to get rid of his mother? My God, I thought. I'm sitting with four murderers? Then I told myself not to be silly; they seemed a nice bunch of men, they didn't look like murderers. Then again, I asked myself, how can you tell? What do murderers look like? I tried to calm myself down by telling myself I was letting my imagination run away with me, but doubts persisted. Why have they brought me here? I thought. Were they going to confess their foul crime to me to ease their conscience? I had made it plain to Greg at the beginning, that I didn't want to hear any details about his criminal past. Now here I was being hoodwinked into listening to it. I don't know what they expected of me. They had no guarantee I wouldn't go running to the law, so what were they going to do to guarantee my silence? Perhaps they would try and implicate me somehow. After all I hadn't been in Garton long, so I didn't know many people here, and certainly not long enough for anyone to give me a character reference.

My next thought was to get out of there. I didn't care what they had done in the past, I didn't want to know any of it. I didn't want them confessing to me. Then I asked myself, what would be the point of them telling me all this if I was going to suffer the same fate as Bill's mother? It didn't make sense, so why were they telling me? What did they want? All sorts of escape plans ran through my mind. I could make the excuse I wanted some fresh air. Yes I thought, that would be my best bet.

My train of thought was broken by Bill continuing with his story. "It didn't take the police long to figure out it was me who had murdered my mother. The operator then showed me a scene of me as a sorry looking individual, whose eyes told of pain and anguish and despair, languishing in a tiny prison cell serving a life sentence."

"This is what you are heading for, Bill," said the operator. "And it doesn't look good, does it?"

"But we never came back to Sandford Valley," I said. "I couldn't have done that terrible thing."

"And you haven't yet," he replied. "You didn't go back to the Sandford Valley mine, because I intervened. Now hear this. If you choose not to go through the process, that is the point you will be returned to, and that will be your fate. Now let me show you something else."

As the scene in front of me unfolded, I found myself in an expensively furnished room. A log fire was roaring up the chimney and a huge beautifully decorated Christmas tree occupied a corner of the large room. I was looking at myself giving Wendy a passionate kiss under the mistletoe with my now grown up children laughing and cheering us on.

"This is how it can be," said the operator. "First you must decide if you are willing to take part in the process. I will advise you accordingly on the outcome of your decision, but for now I want you to relax." He then took me to a room as described by Jason and Rod.

I felt myself give a huge sigh of relief as Bill came to the end of his story. I looked around in case the others had noticed. I inwardly chastised myself for thinking that these four men were about to do me harm. Bill's finale had dispelled that fear.

15

"I was the last to go," said Greg. "The others hadn't returned to where I was, so I had no idea what had happened to them or what to expect. As with the others, the operator led me through that curtain of light and into a cubicle.

Before I tell you about where the operator started from, I am going to take you back to my childhood, simply because I think it has some relevance on my attitude to the world in general, and to women in particular, so here goes

I regarded myself as a pleasant little boy. I wasn't perfect by any means, I did have my moments of tantrums and being obstinate as any growing child does. All in all though, I was an obedient and polite little person who never brought trouble home. Although I say it myself, I had a good head for figures and an aptitude for things mechanical, especially motorcycles. I suppose I had acquired these traits from my father who was considered one of the leading experts on motorcycles. He knew practically every make inside out. Enthusiasts came from all over the country for his expertise, and none ever left disappointed. Although considered one of the best in the country, and could have made himself a wealthy man from his knowledge, he remained virtually a one man operation, having no desire to expand. He never openly said, but I had the idea he never trusted anyone else to handle the valuable machines which were entrusted into his care. Not even I was allowed to touch a customer's beloved machine.

My father was a very clever man, but a disciplinarian, who had the tendency to run his working day to a strict timetable. He would breakfast at precisely 7am, before opening the workshop doors at 8am, not a moment sooner. Work would stop at 10.30am for a brew of tea. My father liked his cup of tea. I don't think he could have got through the day without his brew of tea. The workshop doors would be closed for lunch at 1pm for exactly one hour, and closed again at the end of the working day at precisely 6pm.

I had to earn my place in the workshop as a general dogsbody, fetching and carrying and cleaning parts. It was also part of my job to see that every spanner and wrench was cleaned and put back in its correct place as soon as those workshop doors closed, and woe betide me if anything was missing or out of place. Despite this, my enthusiasm to learn from my father never waned. I gained a wealth of knowledge about motorcycles by just watching him as much as I could. You couldn't keep me away from the place. Apart from school, I spent nearly every waking minute helping out.

Unfortunately when I was only sixteen years of age my father died of cancer. He had been an avid pipe smoker, and apart from eating and sleeping, the Sherlock Holmes style pipe he loved never left his mouth. The smell of his favourite aromatic tobacco and the stink of used oil and grease and petrol fumes would fill the workshop, competing with each other for dominance, which, even today, I can still smell.

I would have loved to carry on the business, I was certain in my own mind I had enough knowledge to have kept the workshop going. My mother though, who was as strict as my father, wouldn't hear of it and dismissed my pleas to keep it going She sold the business, lock, stock and barrel, including my father's three beautiful Harleys, which I had hoped would be handed down to me. I wasn't at all happy with my mother at the time for leaving me nothing to remember him by.

Three years later, she passed away suddenly in her sleep. She hadn't been ill or anything, or at least she had never complained to me about feeling ill, although I had noticed she had slowed down and was not as active as she used to be and had lost some of her sparkle, but I put that down to her age. Being the only child, I inherited what was left, which wasn't a great amount. My mother had got through most of the money from the sale of the business, but there was enough to pay for my engineering course, which I am proud to say I passed with flying colours.

There wasn't a lot of work about in those days, but a vacancy did come up at Blacks Engineering, who manufactured mainly mining equipment. As luck would have it they had a vacancy for an apprentice engineer for which I applied. They were impressed with my qualifications and took me on.

When I reached nineteen-years-old, and this probably sounds conceited, I had grown into quite a good looking lad, and standing at 5' 11" with slim athletic figure and deep blue eyes, I couldn't fail with the ladies, and I was not slow in taking full advantage of this. I didn't care whether they were married or not, it made no difference to me. Some of these encounters produced some very scary moments, and on more than one occasion would find me leaping out of some young married lady's bedroom window, but it only added to the thrill of it all as far as I was concerned. I was 19, and what was life about if you couldn't experience some thrills and spills. I can't count the number of times I had been engaged and on the verge of marriage. I am afraid to say I was a user and made the most of it, and because of my good looks and gift of the gab, I was well able to talk my way out of many difficult situations. I made an art of charming the ladies into bed, but once the challenge of conquering them had been won, I would turn my attention to the next victim.

I suppose it was a case of wanting my cake and eating it, but the unbelievable part about all of this, was deep down it wasn't really what I wanted. You may think having a different girl most nights and going for a drink with the lads when you wanted was a wonderful life. But it's like being so rich you can buy anything you wanted on a whim, which is why the super-rich are bored to tears. There is simply no excitement, no thrill in being able to buy anything you want when you want. The thrill in life is to achieve your desire which you thought would always be out of your reach.

Believe it or not, I often thought about being able to get home after a day's work to find a cooked meal waiting for me, then off to the pub for a drink with the lads, then back home to a loving wife waiting for me to see to my needs. But then the thought of being tied to one person filled me with dread.

The operator had taken me back to the night I met Sylvia. I was to be found, as usual on a Saturday night, with five or six of my friends at the local dance hall, showing off and reminding the lads how many of the girls I knew by skirting around the dance hall chatting them up and deciding who was going to be the lucky girl I would be taking home that night.

My attention was captured by this raven haired beauty as she walked close by with a couple of her friends and sat at a table nearby. I remember thinking she was the most beautiful creature I had ever seen. She was quite tall with a perfect slim figure, and had enormous dark brown eyes. She must have been new in town because I had never seen her or her friends before. I decided there and then she was the one I was going to escort home. I wasted no time in making my way over to where she was sitting. "Would you like to dance?" I asked. She looked up at me with those big brown eyes. "No thank you," she replied, shaking her head.

To be honest I was taken aback. I had not come across a response like this before. I don't think I had ever been refused a dance in my life. In fact most of the girls would come and ask me for a dance. I have to admit my ego had taken a knock, but there was no way I was going to concede defeat. I had a reputation to keep up. I looked about to make sure my friends had not seen the incident and sat down on the seat next to her. "Perhaps we could have a dance later." She looked blankly at me. "Perhaps," she uttered nonchalantly and looked away.

I had my work cut out over the next few weeks getting to know her, but my perseverance paid off, and eventually she gave way to my persistence and let me walk her home. From then on it went from the odd dates to regular meetings.

However, now that the conquest had been won, my wandering eyes were back in action. I will say at this point, I had never cheated on her, but I suppose the point is, it is degrading for one partner to have to endure the other partner's roving eyes. Sylvia though, saw it as part of my makeup and took it in her stride. I would occasionally take it a step to far and we had arguments from time to time and I would stop for a little while only to slide into my feckless ways again, but despite all this, we remained together.

The scene then changed to where Harry and I were having a quiet drink one night. He started a conversation which got me thinking. "You've been with Sylvia a long time now," he said.

"I suppose I have," I replied. "I never thought about it."

"She's lasted longer than most." There was a faint smile on Harry's face.

"What's that look for?" I asked, seeing the amused look on his face.

"Not a wedding coming on is there?"

I didn't answer him. I was busy thinking about Sylvia. Harry's eyes widened. "You are not, are you? I was only kidding. Good grief. Don't tell me the great Don Juan of Garton; Greg Baker has finally been tamed?"

"It's a strange feeling, Harry," I said "I can't get her out of my head. You know me, the one night stand kid. Love 'em and leave 'em. It's different with Sylvia. Her face keeps popping into my head and I get this terrible guilty feeling and I keep going back to her. I have never done that before. The amazing thing about her, is she keeps taking me back, even though she knows what I am like."

"It's love, Greg. The woman loves you, and by the sound of it you are in love with her whether you like it or not."

"I'm going to ask her to marry me this weekend, Harry," I blurted out.

"Not another one," he exclaimed. "How many women have you asked up to yet?"

"I mean it this time. I think it's time I settled down."

I remember Harry looking a bit stunned. "I'll believe that when I see it happen." He grunted. "If I was to be perfectly honest, Greg, I think she is the nicest girl you have ever met. There is no doubt she loves you to bits, but my advice is, don't do it unless you really mean it, I would hate to see her being messed about."

I could hear Harry talking but I wasn't listening. I had made my mind up there and then she was the one for me, and twelve months later we married. It wasn't a big expensive wedding, neither of us wanted a big fuss. Her parents were unable to make the wedding because they had emigrated to Australia a couple of years before, but Sylvia had chosen to stay behind to finish her studies. So quite sensibly she wanted to spend the money getting a house together.

We were fine for about a year. We decided, or I should say, I persuaded Sylvia we should not have children until we had got everything about us. The truth is, I was frightened of being tied down by them. I was enjoying my life as it was and I was free to come and go as I pleased. I didn't want the constraints of children.

Harry's pessimism about me was beginning to come true. I was starting to have itchy feet. I had from the very start had a roving eye, but Sylvia was aware of my past and didn't take any notice. I suppose this gave me licence to do it even more, and I am ashamed to say it led to more than one fling. We had some terrible rows about my infidelity, but to Sylvia's credit she never gave up on the marriage, and I was too much of a coward to leave and fend for myself.

For the next two years the marriage just bounced from one crisis to another. I blamed her for everything, but I know now it wasn't her fault. I couldn't stop my wandering ways, and the more we argued the more I did it. Then one weekend she received some terrible news.

Sylvia had a sister, Brenda, a petite, dark haired bubbly little person, always on the go. She was three years Sylvia's junior and they both got on very well, and as she only lived fifteen miles away, visits were frequent, which I dreaded. Brenda was ok; I got on with her fine, in fact I quite fancied her, but Frank, her husband, wasn't my favourite person. I think he was the most boring human being I had ever met. He would force you to sit and listen to the most awful jokes and then give his stupid guffawing laugh after every one of them. It wouldn't have been so bad if the drink had been flowing, but they were both teetotal, so a visit to the pub was out.

He was a sales manager for a luxury car dealership, and was supplied with a new top of the range car every year which he would come and pose in as soon as it was delivered. In his position, he rubbed shoulders with some of the area's most influential people. A point he never failed to remind us of in every conversation.

Then one August, Sylvia and myself, along with Brenda and Frank, had been invited to join one of Frank's influential friends on a trip across the channel aboard their new motor cruiser. I think his friend was excited to show it off. I suppose it was nice to be invited, but I horrified at the thought of spending two weeks riding the waves in a small yacht unable to escape from boring Frank.

We were to be picked up by Brenda and Frank and driven down to where the cruiser was moored, have a little party, then set off the next day across the channel to France then follow the coastline to the Med. However at the last minute, due to an emergency at work, I was unable to go. Despite me trying to persuade Sylvia to go without me, and promising I would catch up with them in France, she refused. To be honest, another reason besides not wanting to spend two weeks with boring Frank, was the fact that I am no sailor; I won't even take a boat on the park lake. I had been trying to think of excuses not to go, so when this emergency cropped up I heaved a sigh of relief, especially as there were reports of bad weather and heavy seas in the channel.

Despite these reports though, her sister and her husband set sail with their friends across the channel. About half way across they ran into thick fog and collided with a ferry and all aboard the motor yacht were lost, their bodies were never found. An intensive investigation was carried out, which concluded they had strayed off course. Why? remains a mystery. The boat was brand new and had all the latest gadgets and their friend was a competent sailor quite capable of handling his boat in those conditions.

From that day on Sylvia became inconsolable and never recovered from that fateful day. In fact she became worse, descending into a black depression, taking all kinds of pills and hitting the bottle. I didn't help the situation by remarking we'd had a lucky escape. I don't think Sylvia ever forgave me for that. As you can imagine the circumstances devastated her. It is one thing to lose your sibling in an accident, but never finding the body to give them a proper funeral is catastrophic.

I did feel for her, and tried my best to support her, but I wasn't the most compassionate of people, and after months of no response, my patience began to fade. The doctor's had warned me it may be a lost battle, and her refusal to respond began to wear me down. As the months went by, I began to realise the doctor's words were coming true. I was fighting a losing battle against drink and drugs as she refused to come out of that terrible depression.

As I have said, I wasn't the most compassionate of people. I thought if she wasn't going to help herself, then why should I waste my time waiting on her hand and foot? Why should I be trapped into that kind of life? I hadn't got married to carry this burden. Even so there had been great fluctuations in my thinking. There were days when I would willingly have walked out of the door. Then I would stop and reflect what a wonderful woman she had been. I will admit because of my flirtations and frequent drinking, I hadn't been the easiest of people to live with, but she had never given up on me. When push came to shove though, I simply hadn't got her staying power. It's a terrible thing to say, but I would go straight to the pub from work and stay till late hoping she wouldn't be there when I returned home. I don't think she ever realised I wasn't there anyway. In the end I didn't care where she was or what she was doing. She needed help, but I hadn't got the patience to deal with her. I was now at my wits end, spending my time in the pub or in my shed repairing my bikes, anywhere at all to get away from her wailing and drunken rants. When Harry Bains asked me to carry out that inspection at Sandford Valley mine, I pretended to be upset, but if I was to be honest, I was glad. I didn't want to spend any more time in that house than I had to.

The scene changed to where I was just leaving the house to head for the pub. I couldn't stand to be with Sylvia anymore. I know now what a coward I was. She needed help but all I could think of was myself. She pleaded with me not to leave her that night, but I ignored her, slamming the door behind me.

The following scene the operator showed me, filled me with horror. I had been moved on to where I was returning home from the pub a bit worse for wear, I could hear the radio blasting away inside the house as I walked up the drive. I made my mind up there and then I was going to pack a suitcase and leave. I marched into the house and switched off the radio. I was angry, selfishly angry with her for putting me through this. I didn't care anymore about what she was doing to herself. I shook her to waken her, intending to tell her I was no longer prepared to put up with her drinking and foul moods, and then leave. There was no response, so I shook her again harder. Then I realised she was stone cold. I broke out in a cold sweat and panic gripped me as it dawned on me she was dead. I phoned all the services, but even when the doctor pronounced her dead, I refused to believe it. Now she wasn't here, it hit me like a ton of bricks just how much I did love her, but it was too late now.

The next scene made me feel sick. A doctor was bending over my lifeless body and pronouncing me dead. Apparently in a fit of remorse, I had gone on a bender and taken a full bottle of sleeping tablets.

"That isn't going to happen, is it? I gasped.

"What you have just seen will happen," warned the operator. "If you do not alter the course of events. Let me show you how different it can be."

I was suddenly looking along a tree lined avenue. I watched as a large furniture removal van turned into a wide drive and made its way to a large detached house. It was followed by a smart expensive car which came to a halt behind the van. The rear doors opened and two excited young children got out and began running to the house urging Mummy and Daddy to follow. The front doors of the car opened and a man and a woman got out. There was no mistaking it was Sylvia and me. She sidled up to me and gave me a lingering kiss. "It's beautiful," she said, pointing to the house. "We are going to be very happy here."

"What you see is for the taking," said the operator. "It is all down to you. Now let us join the others."

It was here that Greg halted the story. This signalled yet another break. I took advantage of it to draw Greg out of the room. "I know you boys are pouring out your life stories here," I said. "But I'm sorry, Greg, as interesting as they are, I can't see the point of it all, I can't see where this is going."

Greg gave me a wry smile. "I can understand your feelings, but I must ask you to have a bit of patience. We have chosen to tell you our stories from the beginning because they are relevant to the outcome. You will understand why later."

I nodded agreement. "It all sounds very intriguing, and put like that, I can't wait to hear the rest of it."

"As I say," said Greg. "Have a bit of patience. It will be worth it in the end, now there is a lot more to tell, so I think it would be as well if you went home and grabbed a bite to eat and came back later. We can finish this off this evening, that is if it is ok by you."

I said it would be no problem to return later. After all there was only an empty house to go back to, but I did need to run this story through my brain and I didn't want to the continuity of the story to be broken. I shook hands and promised to be back by 7pm.

As I left for home, the sun was about to disappear behind the rolling hills of High Meadows Point, part of a small national park known for its outstanding beauty. The sky had turned a deep orange, tinting a cluster of small black clouds with a golden lining. Under normal circumstances I would have lingered for a while to take in the beauty of this spectacle, but as it was, I only gave it a passing glance. There was too much whirling around in my brain to think of anything else but that bizarre story which had just been related to me by these four men. It is hard to describe the strange feeling I had running through my bones. I felt as though I didn't belong to the world around me, as though I was in a glass box with the rest of the world passing by and I had been spending the day on automatic pilot.

There was no doubt, the story had taken over my mind, which was in turmoil. I wasn't sure whether to believe this fantastic tale or not. Then I asked myself, why would anyone want to make up such a complex story, and for what reason? This part I hadn't yet figured out, but if I was to be honest, I had this gut feeling that the story was perfectly true. I had no reason to believe it not to be, and now there was more to follow. I was quite eager to find out what happened next–in fact I couldn't wait.

16

At 6.35pm I made my way back to Greg's. I had a powerful torch with me because the lane had no lighting at all along its entire length. I stepped out of the door and glanced at the sky to see what sort of night it was going to be. It was as clear as a bell showing a beautiful canopy of stars made all the more brilliant because of the lack of light pollution. A slightly chilly south westerly breeze gave a gentle nudge through the leaves of the Elm trees lining the lane. The world seemed at peace as I strolled leisurely to Harley House, reaching there at about 6.55pm.

All was quiet as I made my up the uneven crazy paved path which led to the kitchen door. If I didn't know better, I would have assumed the place to be deserted. There were no lights showing anywhere from the house, indicating to me that the place was empty. I began to wonder if Greg had fallen asleep when I left and had not yet woken up. However, as I was about to knock on the kitchen door, it slowly swung open and there was Greg holding out his hand to greet me. He led me to a now darkened living room where the rest of them were relaxing. I shook hands with them all, Greg then pointed to the big easy chair I had used earlier. Heavy drapes were now drawn across the window and the only light was from the wood burning stove. Greg remained standing and a silence fell as the others looked to him. It was obvious to me they had been discussing something in my absence, and now Greg was about to reveal what it was.

"The lads, and that includes me, are afraid you may be losing interest." he said. "We are frightened you may be getting a bit sceptical of the whole story. We want to assure you, the experiences we have told you about, and the events which are to follow, are perfectly true. It is imperative you have full confidence in what we tell you, and it is vital you believe in what we say. If you don't, we want you to be honest with us, and say you don't, and we will have to stop it here and now."

I didn't hesitate. "I did have my doubts at first," I said. "You have to agree with me it does take some believing, but having thought about it, I asked myself, why would four strangers proceed to tell me such a fantastic story? It has to be true. I can assure you gentlemen; I truly believe what you are telling me. I have to be honest though, and say I am totally confused as to what the purpose of it all is yet, but I have no doubt it will all become clear very soon, and I am with you all the way."

"We can't tell you how relieved we all are," Greg said "We know it's a lengthy tale and we could have shortened it, but we wanted you to relive the whole thing with us, otherwise you would not have understood the outcome and why it had to be this way, but now I would like to go on."

Greg sank into his chair and continued with the story. "The operator had gathered us all together. "I have now shown each of you the consequences of continuing to tread the paths you are on," he said. "I have also shown each of you an alternative which can be achieved by applying a little more thought to your actions. This part of the process is not compulsory, I can only take you through it if you wholeheartedly consent to it, the choice is yours. I have already explained, that if you do not wish to take part, I will return you to the point at which I intervened and you can carry on your life as it was. Before you make that decision, I will explain what the process is about and what you must do. I will take each of you back through the various stages of your life. I will judge how far back you will go, so hopefully you will have a chance to realise what path your life is taking. There will be one significant point where a vital decision to alter that path will have to be made. You, and only you, must recognise this stage in your life and make the necessary change. Although I know what this vital point is, I cannot help in any way. As soon as you make that change you will be brought back here. Now I must issue a couple of warnings. The change you make must be the correct one and undertaken with the utmost sincerity. Do not try to make changes for changing sake, it has to be that vital one, and if you do it just to please me and not done sincerely, and believe me I will know, you will be judged a failure. The same applies if you miss it, or you refuse to change it, then you will bear the consequences. Secondly I want you to know that although you are repeating parts of your life, you will not realise this and will think it is happening for the first time. I hope you all understand what I am saying?"

"I would like to ask a question," I said. "If we missed these points the first time round, how will we be able to recognise them the second time?"

"A very good question, Greg. I can tell you there will be clues the second time."

"Can you say what form these clues take?"

"Let me put it this way," replied the operator. "Have you ever been somewhere you have never been before, but it all looks familiar? Or met a complete stranger and had a feeling you have met before?"

"I have spoken to many people who have experienced that," I replied. "We call it Déjà vu."

"That experience, Greg, is your brain flagging up an incident in your past life where a different decision or action should have been made and is giving you another chance. Unfortunately almost everybody will dismiss it as coincidence."

"Do you mean all those people who have experienced this Déjà vu thing will have been through a past life?" cried Jason.

"Yes, although they won't realise it of course. Now if there are no more questions, is there any of you who do not wish to go through the process?"

We all looked at Jason. If there was going to be one of us who was going to back out, it would be him, but he was as resolute as any of us to go through with it. "Then we are ready to begin." Said the operator. He once again singled out Jason as the first to go and for the second time they disappeared through that green curtain of light."

"I was terribly nervous," said Jason, taking over from Greg. "Not as nervous as the first time, but I was very uneasy about what the operator was going to show me about myself? I didn't really want to see any more of my pathetic life. Anyway, I seemingly didn't have a choice and we both stepped into that curtain of light. I was confronted by a scene of me being that obnoxious brat playing my parents against each other. This time though I had twinges of guilt about my father always being on the receiving end of it all, but I shrugged them aside and kept on with my little game. As I have said, because of me, my father, unable to stand the atmosphere in the house, took to going out on drinking binges. In the end my mother, without a word, had packed her bags and walked out on both of us. I was very hurt and angry she had not said anything about leaving, or wanting to take me with her, after all I had been on her side and now she had absconded and left me with an alcoholic father who was incapable of looking after me. From time to time I did have feelings of guilt about me being the cause of his decline, but I would brush them aside. It was too late now, his drinking had got the better of him. Just after my fourteenth birthday, he stumbled under the wheels of that passing truck and was killed, and so much for showing compassion, I never even attended his funeral.

I was then shown scenes of myself in a care home hating every minute of it. I got into bad company there, and because of my nagging guilt I had a chip on my shoulder a mile wide. I wanted to hit back at the world for treating me the way it had done. I hadn't the sense to realise it was all my own fault. Encouraged by others I got mixed up in a life of crime and drink and drugs. I was happy to steal from others, my philosophy being, why should they have and not me?

I was treated to scenes of life in the care home I had been sent to. I hated it of course and I was a constant source of trouble. At the age of fifteen I was committed to a young offender's institution. Drug taking, smoking and drinking was rife. I was easily led on by the bigger, older lads. There were times when I knew this wasn't for me. I began to have strong feelings that I had to stop this crazy downward spiral and should have called a halt to it there and then, but I hadn't got the bottle to stand up to the bully boys. It was at this point that I turned to the operator. "This is where I should have stood up to them," I said.

"You were out of control long before then," he answered. "Ask yourself why?"

"I know why," I replied. "My mother deserted me and my father was an alcoholic. I didn't have a very good home-life did I?"

"Listen to yourself," scowled the operator. "It's all me, me, me, and that is the kind of selfish thinking which is leading you to your destruction."

"What do you mean?" I asked.

"You are blaming your indulgence into drink and drugs and crime on a bad home-life."

"Well...err. Yes."

"Ask yourself who caused your parents to argue and eventually part company."

I realised what he was getting at. Had it not been for me playing my parents against each other, things might have been different, and the reason I took to crime and drink and drugs, was because deep down I had a guilty conscience about my father turning to drink which lead to his untimely death.

"Yes I see it now." I said. "I was the cause of it all. If only there was some way I could make peace with my father." I had no sooner uttered those words, when I was suddenly transported to my father's graveside. It was cold and wet. A horrible drizzly rain had soaked through my thin jacket, but I didn't care as I squatted down beside the headstone. I poured out my heart to him, telling him I was bitterly sorry for the heartache I had caused him and I now realised just how much he had loved me and I would always think of him fondly. As I said those words, I knew that these were the things I should have said to him when he was alive. I stood to my feet and bowed my head. "I love you Dad," I said, and turned to walk away. Then I heard a voice from nowhere. "I love you son," it said. I couldn't make up my mind whether I actually heard it, or whether it was my imagination telling me something I wanted to hear. Whichever way, I felt a great burden lift from me.

I was now fast forwarded to when I was nearly eighteen years of age. At this age, if I committed another offence, it would be a prison sentence. Then a stroke of luck came my way. I was pretty good with electronics which fortunately the institution recognised. They managed to get me a placement as an apprentice electrician at Blacks Engineering. I enjoyed the job and worked hard. The institution could see that if I was going to have any chance to better myself, then I should be moved away from the influence of the others. I was given a bed-sit near to the factory. It was very small but the rent was cheap.

I was fast forwarded again. It was the Thursday before the Easter holiday weekend. For some reason I was feeling depressed. I was lonely and needed a good drink and some company. I had decided I would go to see my old friends at the Black Star pub. I had just got ready to go out when Rod came knocking at the door to tell me about the job at the Sandford Valley mine. This was the Déjà vu moment. I had the strangest feeling this had happened before. I promised Rod faithfully I would be at work the next morning, but the lure of a drink with the lads at the Black Star proved too much and before I knew it I was pushing open the door to that foul smelling smoke filled room. I stood for a moment gazing at the sight of half-naked men and women stoned out of their minds slumped across chairs or stretched out on the bare stone floor. Some were trying to dance zombie like to some tuneless music which was screeching at ear splitting levels from the speakers set in every nook and cranny they could find. One of the girls came staggering across and led me to an old settee and pushed me down onto it. She shoved a cigarette into my mouth and lit it and poured me a drink from a huge glass jug then draped herself across me.

That Déjà vu sense hit me again. My God I thought, what on earth am I doing here? Suddenly like a bolt from the blue, I decided that this was no longer what I wanted. It was what I had come out for, but suddenly, not anymore. For once in my life I realised I had been given the chance to escape my crime ridden existence, and by being offered an apprenticeship with good career prospects I had been thrown a lifeline and I was going to grab it with both hands. I pushed the girl away and threw the cigarette to the floor and started to make for the door.

"Where are you going, Jason?" she shouted.

"As far away from here as possible," I shouted back. "This isn't for me anymore."

I pulled open the door to the outside and stepped out straight into that mist. The next thing I know, I found myself being helped from that glass booth by the operator. I had obviously made that crucial decision at the correct time. I next found myself in the relaxing room.

"I was next to go," said Bill. "There were no ifs or buts, the operator came straight to me and took me to the booth and placed me inside telling me to think carefully about his previous talk with us.

I was taken back to where I was in the fish and chip shop and had just seen my mother passing by, arm in arm with another man. My eyes filled with tears in a mixture of anger and sadness. Anger that my mother could be so cruel to my father and sadness that he was being cheated on by her. I returned home in tears. I burst through the door yelling "I've seen her, Dad. I've seen her with another man."

"Calm down son," he said. "Seen who?"

"My mother," I sobbed. "I've seen my mother with another man, they were holding hands, Dad."

There was no reaction from him at that statement. Not a flicker of emotion as he studied my sad contorted face. He eventually pulled me to him and hugged me and told me he had known for a good while. He tried to make a joke of it by saying it served the man right. I thought he would have been devastated, but he was smiling and trying to make a joke out of it. "Let's keep our fingers crossed and hope she runs off with him. What do you say, William?"

I gave a smile but I knew he was putting a brave face on it all. I asked myself time and time again why he let this woman ride roughshod over him? I willed him to fight back, but he rarely did. I got the feeling as I grew older; he thought arguing with her a waste of time because she always had an answer for him.

I was then forwarded to when I was nineteen-years-old and steadfastly refusing to seriously date a girl, but deciding there was nothing wrong in having the odd date or two. I still didn't want any commitments and the girls would have to understand that. There were one or two who tried to get serious, but they were soon got rid of.

Then as you know, at the age of twenty-eight I met Wendy. I fell hook line and sinker for her. What came over me I don't know, but I was smitten with her. The feeling was alien to me, and before I knew what was happening, we were getting married, something I had sworn never to do.

Looking back, Wendy was as near perfection as you could get. I say looking back, because I realise now, though not at the time, I still had issues relating to that torrid time my father and I had with my mother. Each time I thought Wendy was trying to tell me what to do, or what not to do, I overreacted at the thought that I was being controlled. This sort of behaviour had obviously put a strain on the marriage, but not once did she think of leaving me. She loved me and accepted the way I was. She was a wonderful woman, so why couldn't I see that at the time and because I got away with my bad behaviour most of the time, I did nothing to rein it in. Then one day everything came to a head.

I watched as my father became seriously ill. My mother refused to stay home at night to look after him. Eventually he was forced to finish in the coal mine and become reliant on Social Security. That was the signal for my mother to walk out, telling him he was a pathetic excuse of a man and useless to any woman, and he couldn't expect her to live like a pauper. I will never forget those words. Had she said this to him a few years ago, he would still have taken it badly, I'm sure, but if ever there was a time he needed her support it was now. But now things had got tough, she was off to live with her lover, leaving my father to fend for himself. I knew then he wouldn't last very long, she had destroyed his will to live. He died a month later.

It was from this point I began to behave like an idiot, and taking it out on Wendy. Getting revenge on my mother had obsessed me. Wendy got very anxious about me, asking what would happen to her when I was in prison on a life sentence. "One day your mother will get what she deserves, she said. "What goes around comes around."

I shrugged off these pearls of wisdom. They were just words to me and I wouldn't be pacified. I never gave up the search. My mother wasn't going to get away with it. She was going to have to pay dearly for the misery she had heaped on my father. Then as coincidence would have it, on the Thursday before Easter I received the news of my mother's whereabouts.

I confronted Wendy. "I've found her," I growled. "Now she is going to get what's coming to her."

Wendy couldn't believe I was going through with it. She had thought all this ranting and raving about revenge was hot air and I would back down if it ever came to reality. She was absolutely horrified to find I was actually going to carry out my threats.

The operator then forwarded me to that Tuesday night after the mine inspection. I was so consumed with hate for that woman I hadn't even formulated a plan. As Wendy pleaded with me not to go, a voice suddenly entered my head. "Do you really want to lose her, William? Is revenge on your mother worth ruining both your lives for? My father's face appeared in my mind, he was reminding me of what he had said all those years ago when she had left him. "She is unhappy being with me, son, and it makes me unhappy to know she doesn't want to be here, so what is the point of both of us being unhappy? Let her be. Hating her will do you no good."

I suddenly thought of the consequences of what I was about to do. What good would it do if I did kill her? It would only ruin two more lives. The realisation I had to forget all this hatred for my mother hit me between the eyes. She just wasn't worth it, and if I didn't let it go, there would be no future for Wendy or myself. It had already started to come between two people who loved each other very much, and I couldn't allow that happen.

I closed the door and flung my arms around Wendy. "I'm a fool," I said. "From now on I am going to put that woman out of my mind and concentrate on the woman I love." The mist then descended and I was back to the operator.

17

Greg stood to his feet announcing a break of about twenty minutes, which I was glad of. I don't know about the others, but I was in great need of the bathroom. Come to think of it, I don't think I had ever seen any of the others head in that direction. Then again I wasn't waiting outside the door to see who went in and who didn't, it was just one of those strange thoughts which entered my head from time to time and was just as quickly dispatched. I had noticed though, that each time we took a break, the others headed for the kitchen to talk amongst themselves and this time was no exception. Greg must have seen a concerned look on my face and came over to me.

"Don't worry about the lads," he said. "They don't mean to ignore you. In fact we are depending on you more than you know."

"Depending on me?" I repeated. "Why?"

"That is the problem right now. We cannot tell you until we have completed what we have to say. The lads are concerned we are not making our story appear believable."

"You can tell the lads I do believe what they are telling me. Logic tells me that anyone who dares to relate such a mind boggling story must be telling the truth."

"Thank you, Peter. I will tell the boys. You will understand at the end of all this, why we are going to be greatly dependant on you." Leaving me to ponder that statement he turned to Rod. "Tell us what happened to you Rod."

"It seemed like the operator hadn't been gone more than five minutes when he was suddenly back to Greg and me. As with Jason and Bill there was no choice of who would go next. He pointed to me and said, "I'll take you next, Rod." I looked at Greg who just shrugged his shoulders. "First, last or middle," he said. "It makes no difference to me. Hope to see you later." The operator beckoned me to join him at the curtain of light. "Where are Bill and Jason?" I asked. "Are they ok?"

"Never mind Bill and Jason for now," he replied curtly. "You need to concentrate on the task ahead."

I would have been a liar if I told you I wasn't nervous. My stomach was bubbling like a witch's cauldron and his abrupt answer to my question hadn't helped to calm my nerves. Within seconds I found myself in my bedroom with my father who was proceeding to give me the lecture of my life. He had just found out I had broken into the local newsagent with a couple of other lads. My mother was downstairs sobbing her eyes out.

"What on earth do you think you are doing you little wretch?" he yelled. "We didn't bring you up to be a thief. We shall never be able to show our face in town again. Keep away from those lads or you will certainly end up in prison."

I had nothing to say. What could I say? My parents were decent law abiding people and I had let them down. My father threatened to confine me to my room until I pointed out I would be unable to look for work if he did. He relented on his decision and allowed me out in the daytime but I was still confined to the house at night.

I spent months searching for jobs but there was nothing, not the sort of job I wanted anyway. There were plenty of dead end jobs like stacking shelves at the supermarket, or some mind numbing repetitive job on a production line, but I set my mind on being an electrical engineer. I would have loved to go to college but my parents were unable to afford it and I was starting to get depressed about it.

It was while I was on one of my job scouting missions that I was unfortunate enough to bump into Jack, one of the lads I had got into trouble with. He tried his best to get me to join a gang of them who was operating in the town. I did refuse at first, because I knew if I got mixed up with them again I would end up in prison.

Jack was a good talker though, and when he thrust a thick wad of cash under my nose, my dream of going to college flashed before my eyes. My will power faded and I was once again drawn into a life of crime. They started as petty little jobs at first. Then I watched as the operator unfolded a scene of Jack trying to get me to take part in a bigger job and to my horror convincing me that the payoff would be enough to see to my ambition.

I turned to the operator. "This is where I should have said no to him, isn't it?"

"You could have," he replied. "But do you really think it would have altered the consequences of him turning up later in your life?"

I looked at the operator for a moment. What was he getting at? He knew what was going through my mind, but it was obvious he wasn't going to elaborate any more. I was going to have to work this out myself.

"I should have said no to him when I met him in town that day, shouldn't I?"

"As I have said, you could have, but it's not the answer is it? Come on Rod, think about it. Ask yourself why you were tempted."

"That's easy," I replied. "I wanted to go to college and I hadn't got the money and I couldn't get a job.

"Now we are getting somewhere."

"I don't understand," I protested. "There was nothing I could do about it. There were no jobs to go to."

"Are you sure?"

My brain was going into overdrive. It was obviously something to do with my looking for work. "Take me back to when I was looking for work," I pleaded. I was convinced the answer must be there somewhere. In a flash I was back pounding the streets looking for work. I was confused. I know I had tried almost every electrical engineering firm there was but with no results. Had I missed one? I retraced my steps but the result was the same. "There just aren't any jobs," I said to the operator.

"Are you absolutely certain?" he asked.

"Of course I am," I replied irritably. "You know I spent hours and hour's loo..." It suddenly dawned on me what he had been trying to say to me. There *were* jobs to be had. There were no engineering jobs available, but there were other jobs. Dead end jobs as I called them, but at least I would be earning money. The simple decision now to take one of those jobs would alter the whole course of my life and would enable me to save for my education, plus if I had taken one of those jobs I wouldn't have been wandering the streets, which would have eliminated that disastrous encounter with Jack.

"Well done Rod," said the operator. "You have now made that vital life changing decision. We can now return."

18

Greg eased himself out of his chair. "Thank you for that gentleman. That just leaves me to tell my story. If you are in agreement, Peter. We would like to finish off what we have to tell you this evening. It may be a bit late when we are through."

As it was to be a holiday the next day, it didn't matter how late it was. I said it was no problem for me.

Greg settled back in his chair. "Like the others," he began. "I was nervous. I couldn't ask the others because they had never returned to the room. I had no doubt they were safe and sound, but it would have been a help to have some insight as to what to expect. Anyway it was too late to back out now, not that I had any   intentions of doing so.

Before I knew it, the operator had led me through that curtain of light. The mist cleared and I found myself, drink in hand, in the local dance hall with some of my friends. We were as usual being our boisterous selves. I was at the same time eyeing up the girls and trying to choose the lucky one who I would be taking home that evening. Little did I know I was destined to meet Sylvia.

I was in the process of telling a funny story when my flailing arm caught the tray of drinks Sylvia was carrying as she tried to pass. I apologised a thousand times and replaced the spilt drinks. From then on there was no other girl in the room. I thought her the most beautiful girl I had ever seen.

The operator then decided to move me on. My impression was that he was reminding me of how I had adored Sylvia when we first met. Now he had fast forwarded me to when we were married. Regretfully I still had my roving eye. Up till then I had remained faithful, but I was weakening. Sylvia was too blasé about my flirting and I did it openly, knowing she would just laugh it off. I took this as a licence to have more serious encounters.

Despite my philandering there was only one issue where we didn't see eye to eye. Sylvia wanted children but I didn't. Kids tied you down too much, which I didn't want. I didn't tell her that of course, I just simply kept putting it off by saying we weren't ready yet.

The operator moved me on again. Sylvia and I had been invited by her sister and her husband to join them aboard their friend's yacht for a two week sailing holiday. I had never seen Sylvia so excited. She loved boats of any kind and she was looking forward so much to this holiday of a lifetime with the additional interest of being with her sister.

I was dreading it. Sailing just isn't my choice of holiday. I might have been persuaded to try a cruise on some big liner, but bouncing up and down on the sea on a small yacht, especially with that boring brother-in-law of mine, was not my idea of a good time. I tried to think of a good excuse not to go, but I could think of none Sylvia would accept.

Then the day before, I received a life-saving phone call. There was an emergency at work. To be honest, I didn't have to go. I was always the first one to be contacted in an emergency, but if I had said I couldn't make it, there wouldn't have been a problem, they would simply have contacted the next one down the chain. This was my chance though. This was the excuse I had been waiting for, and being the selfish oaf I was, I accepted. Sylvia was devastated. She had been looking forward so much to this holiday. I did feel a bit mean, but I was so pleased I had got out of it, that it overrode any guilty feelings I had. Three days later, we received news of the tragedy at sea involving the yacht. The consequences that followed you know about. I could feel the operator's eyes on me. I knew this was the point at which I had to make a decision. "I should have turned that job down and gone on that holiday, shouldn't I? " I said.

The operator looked at me for a minute. "I can give you one clue. I did tell each of you, that you have to alter the course of your life. I have shown you a section of your life that contains the point at which you have to make that decision. Now, do you think the decision you have just mentioned will do that?"

Obviously not, I thought to myself. I was beginning to panic. "Is it my selfishness," I asked. "Should I have made more effort to stop being selfish?"

"You're on the right track," he replied.

Ok, I thought to myself. It's something to do with my selfish attitude, which I confess is a pretty wide area. Is it my unfaithfulness? This is one thing I would be stopping, but I can't see stopping that would   alter anything dramatically. Is it going out drinking and leaving Sylvia on her own? It would be good to stop doing that but I am certain that is not the answer. What else have I been selfish with? Well Sylvia did want kids and I didn't. Wait! That's it. I should have started a family. Having kids would certainly have altered our lives. We would certainly have trodden a different path. With a family we wouldn't have been asked to go on that cruise, and it's a fifty-fifty chance the cruise may never have happened. Even if it had gone ahead and the boating accident had happened, although Sylvia would have been devastated by the accident, she would never have turned to alcohol. She would have remained strong for the children.

"That's it," grinned the operator. "That is the correct decision. Now it is time to return to the others."

Greg rose from his chair. "Let's take a break for fifteen minutes before we continue."

I agreed to that. I needed to stretch my legs. All sorts of things were running through my head as I used the bathroom, but nothing I could make sense of. The only sensible thing to do was to let the story run its course and then perhaps the picture would be clearer. I returned to my seat. No one else had stirred. "Is there much more to this story?" I said.

Greg shook his head. "Not a lot more. We should reach the conclusion soon."

"I'm intrigued to find out what part I have to play in all this," I said.

"All in good time," he replied. "We were all now gathered before the operator." continued Greg. He apologised for worrying us by separating us, but insisted it was necessary."

"I didn't want any of you voicing your experiences with each other," he said. "It would have been unhelpful in your life changing decisions. You each had to genuinely recognise you were treading the wrong path, and also recognise that vital moment in your life where you could put it right. I did give a little help, but I am pleased to say you all made those vital decisions by yourselves."

"So what happens now?" asked Rod. "Are we going to start our new lives again?"

"Yes, you will be returned to start your lives and to follow your new path. Let me warn you though. Anyone who had failed to bond with their fellow species the first time, like yourselves, are all given a second chance. If you start to stray from the new direction you have been offered, and return to your old ways," He pointed to the thousands of wisps of light dashing across the void in all directions. "You will become one of those spirits endlessly gathering information for eternity."

"Let's get started then," said Jason. "I can't wait to get into my new life."

"Not so fast," replied the operator. "There is something you must do first."

Greg suddenly fell silent. I looked up to see he had his eyes fixed on me. It was as though he was nervous about proceeding with the story. I looked around and found the rest of them had fixed me with that sort of nervous stare.

"What is it?" I asked.

"This is where we need your help, Peter."

"Just ask away," I said. "Whatever it is you want me to do, I will do it. I have told you before, you can trust me."

Greg nodded. "Thank you, Peter. I err...."

"Spit it out Greg. If I can possibly help you, I will."

Greg handed me an envelope with the name Charlie Maple written on the front. "We want you to contact this man and give this to him."

"We used to be good friends," said Bill. "We want him to organise a search party to go down the Hays Heath Mine. There is a note telling him to go to Mannings Drift and the exact location to look."

"What are they looking for?" I asked.

"Sorry," apologised Greg. "We can't tell you that just yet."

"I don't understand. I will do all I can to help, of course I will, but why don't you go to this Charlie yourselves? Why do you want me to go?"

"We can't," said Rod. "Or we would. I'm sorry, Peter, but it has to be you."

"We are sorry to spring it on you like this, " apologised Greg. "We know you are finding it a bit confusing, but it will all become clear later, and you will begin to understand why we had to start our story from the beginning. We have searched a long time to find a person we could trust, and who would believe in us. Trust me, now you are in full possession of all the facts, all the pieces will eventually fit together. If we had just sprung this on you in the beginning, you would have laughed in our faces and walked away. Now we are putting our faith in you to find this man."

"Well I can't say I understand what's going on," I said. "I still don't understand why you can't contact him yourselves, but I will see if I can find him. Goodness knows what I'm going to say to him mind you. He is going to want to know how I came by this envelope, what am I going to tell him?

"You will think of something I'm sure," said Bill. "Charlie is an intelligent man; he will listen to what you have to say."

"Which is nothing at the moment," I replied. "I suppose I will think of something though."

"We are in your hands now, Peter. Our new lives depend on you. There is one more thing we have to ask of you."

"Oh, and what is that?"

"You must promise not to tell anyone about what has gone on here. You must keep this to yourself. You have never met us, do you understand?"

I stuffed the envelope into my inside pocket and rose to my feet. "I won't tell anyone, you have my promise on that. I doubt anyone would believe me anyway." I said my goodbyes to them all and wished them well.

I couldn't remember the walk home. My head was buzzing with the events of the day. I had become deeply suspicious of what they were asking, and a million and one questions were racing through my mind. Why couldn't they contact this Charlie Maple themselves? To say it had to be me was highly suspect. And why were they so insistent on me remaining tight lipped about what had gone on in that house? And where did the other three keep appearing from? I became increasingly convinced they must have been hiding in the house all the time, and what was it they were looking for they couldn't tell me about? Something didn't ring true. I decided they were up to something and it looked to me as though this Charlie was in on it. For some reason they needed a gullible person to let him know they were ready to carry out the next part of their plan. I racked my brains trying to fathom what it was they were up to. The conclusion I reached from the last part of their story was that they had got something hidden in that mine. Could it be a haul of drugs I wondered, or the proceeds of a bank robbery? What better place to store it than in an abandoned part of a mine.

I had to admire them, it was a very elaborate story they had plied me with to get me into their confidence. I couldn't understand why they had to cook up such an incredible story, but I suppose the logic tells me, the more unbelievable a story is, the more you tend to believe it. That's how conmen gain your confidence, isn't it? And to give them their due, they had very nearly succeeded.

I should have given Greg his envelope back and walked away there and then. I did tell Greg when we first met that I didn't want to become involved in any illegal goings on, but now I had an insatiable curiosity to find out what their little scheme was. Whatever it was, the end result must be worth it to them.

I must have slept well that night despite having my mind in turmoil, because I awoke feeling very refreshed. Questions were still running through my brain, but I knew the only way to get answers was to find this

Charlie Maple. I made myself some breakfast and did a bit of tidying up. I was in the middle of this, and my thoughts were on yesterday's events when the phone rang. It was Jane.

"Peter where on earth have you been? I tried to phone you several times yesterday but got no answer."

"It's been absolute mayhem at work," I replied. "I was shattered when I got home on Saturday night. I just had some supper and went straight to bed. Then I spent yesterday with Greg."

"Who's Greg?"

"He lives in that house at the end of the lane."

"I thought that place was empty?"

"I thought so too, but it's not."

"I tried to phone you about 9.30 last night but got no answer."

"I was still with Greg."

"Whatever were you doing at that time of night?"

I hesitated to give an answer. I was between a rock and a hard place wasn't I? I wanted to unload my suspicions on her about those four, but I had promised not to tell. What the heck I thought, I have to confide in someone, and I knew I could trust her with my life. If she promised not to tell, then she wouldn't. Anyway it wasn't necessary to repeat the whole story.

"I had a strange day with him yesterday," I said. "There were another three at the house when I arrived."

"So what was strange about that?"

"Well, these three seemed to have turned up from nowhere. He's never mentioned them all the while I have been helping him with his motorbikes."

"Surprise visit maybe," suggested Jane.

I shook my head. "No they came with a purpose."

"What makes you say that?"

"They related some fantastic story to me. It took them all day until late last night. I still can't grasp why."

"What story?"

"It doesn't matter. I don't believe it anyway. In a nutshell they want me to find somebody by the name of Charlie Maple and give him an envelope. They want him to organise a search party to go down some coal mine not far from here."

"Who is this Charlie Maple, and what is it they are looking for?"

"That's just it. They say they can't contact him themselves and they won't tell me what it is that's down there."

"Sounds very strange to me."

"It's highly suspicious. If you ask me there is something dodgy going on."

"What are you going to do?"

"I'm going to try and find this Charlie Maple."

"I'd forget it if I were you. I think you have got enough on your plate with that job of yours. It doesn't sound as though you have much time to yourself like you used to have." I groaned inwardly. She was going to nag me about my job. "I did try to warn you about that job, Peter." She continued. "They are not going to pay you that kind of money for a nine to five job are they? You will be expected to practically live at work."

"Don't exaggerate, Jane. It's not that bad."

"Oh really. I bet you have worked late every night this week."

"Yes I have, but don't forget I am now responsible for the sales of the whole group, and it's just at this particular time it's been busy with the Easter sales."

"Yes, then it will be the Whitsuntide sales, then the summer sales, then the winter sales and God knows when I would see you at Christmas. Meantime Jane here would be at home sucking her thumbs. What kind of life would that be for me?"

"You are not thinking straight," I said. "You have to look at the long term benefits. The extra money will bring nice secure future and you will be able to live in a nice big house in relative comfort."

"Oh yes, very nice," she replied sarcastically. "And who will be in this nice big house with me? It won't be you, will it?"

That was it. I could feel my temper rising at this silly woman who consistently refused to listen to reason. I was doing this for us, why couldn't she see that? "I'm not going to listen to any more of this negative rubbish," I barked. "Ring me when you are prepared to talk sense." With that I slammed down the phone.

I stood by the phone for a moment trying to calm down my anger. It was very rare I lost my temper. I was usually pretty even tempered and maybe I shouldn't have slammed the phone down on her and perhaps I should ring her back. Then I thought, no, why should I? It was Jane who was being negative. It's up to her not me.

The phone rang again. There you go I thought, she's come to her senses. I picked up the phone. "Hello."

"It's Jane, Peter. I don't want you to say anything, just let me speak."

"Ok go ahead," I said feeling a little smug.

It is obvious to me Peter, you think more of that job than you do your family. We have told you our concerns and you have ignored them. I cannot carry on like this anymore. I need my man around me, but my man is now married to his job and the money it brings. You have no intentions of giving it up and I have no intentions of living like a recluse. Therefore, Peter, I think we have reached the end of the road. I won't be in contact again and please do not contact me unless you are prepared to have a change of heart. Goodbye and take care."

The line went dead. The anger had now returned. I slammed down the receiver. How dare she blame it all on me? Well, if that's what she wants then so be it. I decided to have a stroll to the Kings Arms. Perhaps a good walk and a couple of drinks would calm me down a bit.

As I was putting on my Jacket I thought about the envelope which Greg had given me. Perhaps I could open it up and see what was inside and seal it back up. I fished in my jacket pocket where I had put it, but it wasn't there. I searched every pocket but found nothing. I even searched my other jacket which was hanging on the next peg, but discovered only empty pockets. I couldn't figure it out. I was sure I had put it in this jacket pocket. I must have dropped it somewhere I thought. The only other alternative was that I had left it on the table at Greg's. I decided to call round there on my way to the Kings Arms just to make sure.

19

It was about 11.45 am as I put on my jacket and stepped through the door to take myself off to the Kings Arms. The sky was clouded over but it didn't look as though it would rain. The air was decidedly cooler than it had been, but it wasn't so cold you had to wrap up. I changed my mind though and opted to switch my jacket for a raincoat just in case the weather changed and it decided to rain after all.

I closed the gate after me and made my way to Harley House. The journey would kill two birds with one stone. I could see if I had left the envelope behind last night and could let Greg know I was going to go for a drink and perhaps I could persuade him to come with me. I deviously thought I may be able to squeeze more information out of him and make sense of what was going on.

I pushed open the rusting gate of Harley House and studied the neglected exterior of the house. I couldn't make out whether it was my imagination or not, but the place seemed even more dilapidated than usual. It was deathly quiet. Not even a tweet of a bird could be heard.

I made my way up the crumbling pot holed filled drive to the kitchen door. This time though there was no one to greet me. I rapped loudly on the door but there was no answer. I listened for any movement inside the house, but it was deathly quiet. I lifted the latch on the door expecting it to be locked, but the door slowly creaked open. I stood there for a moment staring into the kitchen. "Are you there, Greg?" I shouted. There was no reply. I stepped slowly inside and stood surveying the kitchen. I couldn't believe what I was seeing. That old fashioned but tastefully decorated neat and tidy kitchen I had been to on my recent visits, was now a gloomy, dust laden, cobweb covered room. That lovely old chunky pine table which dominated the middle of this large kitchen was now badly stained and mildewed and thick with dark grey dust. The matching chairs were scattered about the place, most with missing or broken legs. I made my way into the living room. The scene was similar to the one in the kitchen. Those easy chairs we had used for our meetings were now scattered at all angles about the room.

The ornately patterned covers were unrecognisable under a thick mantle of dust. Huge cobwebs hung from every nook and cranny in the room, and those once beautiful red velvet drapes now hung haphazardly from the few hooks left to support them.

I must have stood there for a good ten minutes visualising the room as it had been. I could see us all sitting around in a semi-circle while each one related their stories. How on earth had it got into this state?

Then my brain clicked into gear. They were playing it safe, weren't they? They had abandoned the house, making it look as though no one had been there for years in case I cottoned on to their dubious plans and had gone to the police instead. Which is what I should have done in the first place. Right now though I was playing detectives and I was enjoying it. Besides, if I could find out exactly what they had stored in that mine, and when they were going to collect their ill-gotten gains, it would give the police a head-start. I had to try and find this Charlie Maple which would involve a visit to the town hall. I couldn't do that until Tuesday of course, so right now it was the Kings Arms for a couple of drinks. I made my way out of the house, closing the door behind me and made my way to the pub.

The Kings Arms was quite busy. There were even some hardy customers seated outside in the garden area. I made my way to the bar. I was quite thirsty after my brisk walk from Harley House.

"Hello, Peter," chirped Tom the landlord. "Haven't seen you for a while."

It was on the tip of my tongue to say I had been at Harley House but I had promised never to mention my meetings there."

"I've been busy at the new store," I said.

Tom thought for a moment. "The last time you were in here Old Walter and Ben were trying to persuade you to keep pigeons. I thought it was quite funny. I thought they had scared you off."

"I remember that," I said.

"They are over there, shall I call them over?" He let out a chortling laugh.

"Don't you dare," I protested. I didn't want to get involved in discussing pigeons again. I decided to change the subject quick. "Tell me, Tom," I said. "Do you know much about that house at the end of meadow lane?"

"Do you mean Harley House?"

"Yes that's the one."

"Don't know much about the place. I know it's been empty for about twelve months, why, is it up for sale?"

"No I don't want to buy it. I was just interested in its history. It's a shame such a large house is standing empty."

"Well I know the bloke who used to live there had a collection of Harley Davidsons. Worth a fortune I believe, that's why it's called Harley House. Now what was his name... err Black... Barker... Baker! That was it, Greg Baker, he worked for Blacks engineers as an electrician then he just suddenly disappeared. If I remember right, that was an Easter weekend. Don't know what happened to his motorbikes. I wouldn't have minded one myself though."

"Oh," I said, trying to sound surprised. "Just disappeared did he?"

"Not only him," said Tom. "There were three others as well. I can't remember their names offhand."

"So what happened?"

Tom shrugged his shoulders. "I don't know the details. It was before I came to Garton to take this place on. All I know is, it was something to do with one of the mines around here. Charlie Maple is the man to ask, he's in charge of both Sandford Valley and Hays Heath mine. He'll tell you what happened."

My heart skipped a beat. What a coincidence that Tom knew this man. I couldn't believe my luck. It seems Charlie Maple and I were about to cross paths. My mind was racing. The pieces of the jigsaw were fitting together very nicely. I was convinced these five had pulled off some big job. Something so lucrative they had to hide their spoils for a year until the heat was off. I'd bet anything there was a huge stash of drugs hidden down Hays Heath mine and who would disbelieve the manager of the mine telling the story of the four men disappearing, feared lost underground in Sandford Valley. Of course he knew the search parties would find nothing, because they were never there to start with, they had never gone down the Sandford Valley mine. Come to think of it there may have been more than five of them to carry out this plan. Probably not the winding man at Sandford Valley, he couldn't see who was riding the cage. Bill could have signalled an empty cage to descend, but somehow I suspect the winding man at Hays Heath was in on it. How else could Charlie have arranged for the four to be taken down Hays Heath with their ill-gotten gains. Charlie wouldn't have been able to go with them because with the opening ceremony going on at Sandford Valley he had to show his presence there.

For that reason, Charlie wouldn't have known exactly where the haul had been hidden. He wouldn't have dared make contact or visit Harley

House himself in case he was seen, which would have raised awkward questions. He would have to wait until they contacted him. There was no hurry anyway, nobody would ever find it, and if the police were still looking for it, the intensity of their search would have waned a little now.

As I saw it, these four had been waiting until a complete stranger came along. Someone gullible enough to be taken in by their incredible story, and be persuaded to contact Charlie, and it looked as though they thought I was that person. I must admit, that if it wasn't for their story about it having to be me to make contact with this Charlie Maple not ringing true, I might have fallen for it. Well, hard luck boys, I thought to myself, Mr gullible has just figured out what you are up to, and you are going to get the shock of your lives.

"Where can I find him?" I asked.

"He's captain of our darts team. He'll be in tonight for our annual Easter darts knockout competition. Are you interested, Peter? It isn't too late to enter, it's only ten pounds a man. "

I declined of course. I had never played darts in my life. Who knows where those darts would have ended up when they left my grasp. "You would have to have an ambulance standing by when it was my turn," I laughed. "I might just as well give you the money and sit and watch."

I was delighted in having found this Charlie Maple so quickly and was chomping at the bit to meet up with him that evening. I now had to plan how I was going to approach this man. I had to be careful what I said. I was going to have to ask questions, but I didn't want him to get suspicious or I might blow the whole thing.

20

At about 7.15pm I set off for the Kings Arms, taking the route past Harley House. I knew it would be deserted, but all the same, I had a compulsion to take myself past it. As I reached the gate, I stood for a couple of minutes staring up at the house hoping against hope there would be some sign of life, but it was deserted as I expected it would be. These four had flown the nest, hadn't they? They had gone   into hiding somewhere, presumably until Charlie contacted them.

I arrived at the Kings Arms about 7.40pm. As I opened the door to the bar I could see the darts match was well under way. The atmosphere was one of hushed silence, punctuated at intervals by sharp intakes of breath and the odd word of encouragement from the spectators seated at their drinks laden tables around the dartboard. I almost tiptoed my way to the bar and ordered my favourite drink.

"Is Charlie in?" I asked.

With his hands full pulling my pint, Tom nodded across the room. "See the chap on the scoreboard? That's him. Wait until the competition is finished and I will introduce you."

I glanced across to the scoreboard to see a broad beamed man who looked to be in his late fifties. He was, I would say about 5' 9" to 5' 10" with a thick mop of dark greying hair.

After a couple of hours there was a loud cheer and lots of handshaking and the wrappers being torn from the sandwiches and sausage rolls. The man in question headed towards the bar.

"Who's won it then Charlie?" asked Tom.

"Salty, who else?" grunted Charlie.

Tom looked at me. "He wins it nearly every year."

"Glad he's on the darts team though," said Charlie, pointing to a huge engraved silver trophy in a glass cabinet. "Thanks mainly to him, we've been champions of the darts league for the last five years."

"He must be pretty good," I said. "He should turn professional."

"He did think about it," replied Charlie. "But decided there was too much pressure."

"This is Peter, by the way" said Tom. "Peter, meet Charlie. Peter has come in specially to meet you, Charlie. "

We shook hands. "Pleased to meet you." I said. "I would like a word with you if you are not too busy."

He looked at me for a minute, his eyes burrowing into mine. There was an unmistakable look of curiosity in his eyes. "Oh," he said. "About what?"

"Well, it's a bit delicate. Can we go somewhere a bit quieter?"

"Go in the lounge bar," said Tom. "There isn't anyone in there."

We made our way into the lounge bar and settled at a table. Almost immediately Charlie pounced. "Now what's this all about?" he asked.

I had to gather my thoughts quickly. My first impression of Charlie was of a straightforward not to be messed about person. As the General Manager over two mines, he was obviously very intelligent and used to dealing with all kinds of people, so he wasn't going to be taken in by any old story. I had to try and pry information from him without raising suspicion that I was on to them.

"It's very difficult," I replied. "I don't know where to start."

"Well the answer, as always, is to start at the beginning."

"Before I do," I said. "I want you to know I am no nutcase, I want you to believe what I am going to tell you."

His brow furrowed and he sucked hard on his pipe sending a plume of smoke spiralling towards the ceiling. "You had better tell me what's on your mind, Peter."

I had a dream the other night," I started. "It was so real. I can't get it out of my head."

"A dream?" he grunted. "You have dragged me over here to tell me about a dream."

"I know it sounds strange, but please hear me out."

"Go on," He sighed. "I'm here now."

"I found myself in that empty house at the top of Meadow Lane."

"Harley House you mean?" interrupted Charlie.

"Yes, that's the place. I was talking to these four guys. I didn't know who they were, but I gathered they were miners."

I noticed Charlie's face had visibly paled. "What makes you think they were miners?"

"Well, Sandford Valley, that new mine up the road came into the conversation, and there was another mine mentioned, it was err... now what was it called? Heath something."

Charlie sat bolt upright in his seat. "Hays Heath," he snapped. "Was it Hays Heath?"

"Yes," I said. "That was it. Do you know it?"

Charlie's eyes narrowed. "And you say this was in a dream?"

"Yes," I said. "It was so weird."

"Why the dream about that house?"

"That's just it. I don't know. I don't know anybody who lives there. I have never seen anybody there."

"That's because nobody lives there," Charlie almost growled.

"You see," I said. "That makes it even weirder, doesn't it?"

Charlie emptied his glass and stood to his feet. "I need another drink."

I needed another so I offered to refill his glass. I could see from his penetrating stare I had already raised his suspicions. I had to be careful how I proceeded from here. I didn't want the story to sound ridiculous. I returned with the drinks.

"What happened in this dream?" asked Charlie. "And why are you telling me all this?"

"This is the unbelievable bit," I said. "One of the guys was called, Bill"

"My God," murmured Charlie.

"Are you ok?" I asked.

"Yes, yes, just carry on."

"Well, he told me to find a Charlie Maple and tell him to take a search party down the Hays Heath mine and search in the old man's drift near to where they were going to join the Sandford Valley mine."

"Old Manning's drift," butted in Charlie. "It's the Old Manning's drift."

"That could have been it. Well, I had to write down what I could remember the next morning, but I didn't think any more about it until Tom mentioned your name. He said you were a friend of one of the men who had gone missing. I had to contact you of course. It's too much of a coincidence not to have some meaning to it, don't you think?"

Charlie lapsed into silence. He just sat and stared into the glass. He then looked up at me his eyes burrowing into my brain. "What do you know about those four?" he asked.

"I'm sorry, I don't know what you mean. I don't know anything about them. It was just a dream."

"You must have read about them somewhere, to dream about them."

"Are you telling me they are real people?" I must admit I sounded convincingly surprised.

Charlie's eyes again burrowed into mine. "Yes they are real, or should I say they *were* real."

"Wow," I gasped. "This is getting more bizarre by the minute. I don't know anything about them. I'm new around here. I've only just come to live in the area. Who are they? What happened to them?"

There was no answer from him, he emptied his glass and started towards the bar. "I'm getting another drink," he indicated to my glass. "Do you want another?"

"Yes but I'll get..."

He ignored my offer and disappeared into the bar, reappearing a few moments later with fresh drinks, thrusting one in front of me.

"Do you know the new Sandford Valley mine about five miles from here?" he asked.

"I know of it," I replied. "I have never been there."

"Well, it was finished and ready for the official opening which was going to be on Easter Monday last year. On the Friday, Bill, Greg, Rod and a young lad named Jason, who was Rod's apprentice at Blacks engineers, had gone underground to make sure all the machinery was in order and ready for the grand opening. Well, they never came up again. Search parties were sent down and searched every inch of that mine, but there was no sign of them. It was a new mine, so there were only straight cut roads to search. There were fears they had been trapped, or buried by a roof collapse, or they had walked into a patch of gas, but there had been no roof   collapses or the slightest trace of gas. They even dragged the sump at the shaft   bottom but they had mysteriously vanished into thin air."

"Fascinating story," I said. "What do you think happened to them?"

"We don't know. Nobody has ever come up with an explanation."

"Do you think they could have come out without anyone knowing?"

"They couldn't possibly have done. When they went down, they decided to inspect the lower level first. We know they completed that part because, Harry, the winch man received the signal to take them up to the first level. The cage remained there waiting for the signal to bring them up when they had finished inspecting the top level, but the signal never came. After a few hours the winch man became concerned that they should have completed their inspection a long time ago and raised the alarm. When I arrived at the mine, the cage was still at the top level waiting for me to give the word to raise it. It was empty of course when it reached the top. That is when a search party was organised.

Charlie took a large gulp of his beer and remained silent, staring into his drink. "You must have read the story of those four somewhere," he said finally.

"I didn't," I protested. "I didn't know about any of this until today. I was asking Tom about the house and he told me the guy who lived there had vanished, but he didn't know any more than that. But even if I had read the story, I couldn't have possibly known about Manning's drift, could I?"

Charlie stared hard at me then shook his head. "I don't know what to believe. You realise what you are asking, don't you? You want me to persuade the authorities to organise a search party to go down Hays Heath looking for four men that didn't even go down that mine, all on the strength of a dream. They will think I have lost the plot."

"I know it sounds crazy, but as the manager you must have some influence."

"But they went down Sandford Valley. What has Hays Heath got to do with it?"

"I have no idea, I am only telling you what happened in my dream. It must have some significance though. Is it possible they found a way through from one mine to the next?"

Charlie shook his head. "No," he said firmly. "We were going to join up into Manning's drift, but decided against it. We thought it too dangerous because of the gas that tends to build up in old workings."

"You mean blackdamp?"

"You know about blackdamp then?"

"It was mentioned in my dream. Bill said something about blackdamp."

"What? What did he say about it?"

"I can't remember. It was just one of those words that stuck in my head."

Charlie fell silent again. I could almost hear the cogs turning in his head. "Are you sure you don't know anything about those four?"

"I'm positive. I had almost forgotten about this dream until I heard your name mentioned."

"Have you been to the house?"

"Yes I go past it quite a lot, why?"

"Have you ever seen anyone there?"

"No, it looks completely deserted. You don't think someone is in there do you?"

"No of course I don't. If you want my honest opinion, Peter, I think you are reading too much into this dream. I can't help thinking, that despite you saying you haven't, you must have read something about this somewhere and it has played on your mind, hence the dream. You can't get away from the facts. Twelve months ago, these men went down the Sandford Valley mine and never came up again, that fact we are certain about because the cage never returned to the surface. A search was conducted and nothing found. Take my advice, Peter and forget all about it."

I had a feeling I had got Charlie rattled. He was probably thinking I was getting a little too close for comfort. It was obvious to me there were more people involved, but at this particular moment I wasn't interested in them whoever they were. Charlie was the kingpin and he was my target.

I could see I wasn't going to get any further with him for now. His barriers had gone up and that was that. Pressurising the man was not the answer. My best chance was to remain friendly towards him. I shook him by the hand and thanked him for listening. I assured him I would be taking his advice and forget about the whole thing. That was what I was telling him, but deep down there was no way I was going to do that.

21

I was at a stage now, where I wanted to keep an eye on Harley House in case I had panicked Charlie Maple into taking a chance to contact Greg and Co. I couldn't do this without staking the place out every night. Now this sort of activity is all very well in films, but not so exciting in reality. There is certainly nothing glamorous about hiding behind a hedge, along a pitch black lane on a freezing cold night for hours on end, listening to some funny noises going on around you. You start to think all sorts of things to pass the time. I was even having a conversation with myself at times.

"I think you are letting your imagination run away with you," I argued with myself one night. "I mean, think about it. Is this man, this Charlie Maple, who is a manager over two mines, going to risk a well-paid job and a dream pension by getting involved in stuff like that? It doesn't make sense."

I must admit, if anyone else had presented me with a tale like that, I would have dismissed it as nonsense. But then I couldn't help thinking there was something to it. Why did these men want Charlie to search Hays Heath mine?

I was fortunate enough to be able to grab a few days holiday. The firm was so delighted with the way I had handled the Easter sales, they were only too pleased to grant me some time off, this gave me the perfect opportunity to do a bit of detective work.

I decided that the local library was the place to look up the report of the incident in the newspapers at the time of the men's disappearance. There was a big splash in the local newspaper, but only one of the nationals reported it, and that was relegated to a short column in one of the inside pages, which is why I had never come across the story. Consequently, the newspapers didn't tell me any more than I already knew. They only repeated what Charlie Maple had told me. My nightly spying missions at Harley House were also fruitless. The only movement to travel the lane at night besides myself were a couple of Badgers on their nightly forage for food.

Despite not making progress, I still had it in mind that Charlie Maple was mixed up in whatever was going on. In fact I was so convinced my contact with him would spur him into some kind of action, I took to spying on him. It didn't last long though. After spending hours tailing him on foot, or sitting in my car, or hiding behind some garden wall watching him snuggle down by the fire while I froze to death outside, I decided playing at detectives wasn't for me. However I didn't give up. I was determined to get to the bottom of whatever it was they were up to. In the end I decided to go to the police with my suspicions and let them do the detective work.

As you would expect I was as nervous as ever as I entered the police station that morning. My stomach was bubbling like a pan of porridge on the hob. I had changed my mind a dozen times on the way there. They weren't going to believe my story, were they? Even Jane had dismissed it out of hand, and she knew I was not given to making up such tales, so how was I going to get the police to believe me?

There were some funny facial expressions as I told the desk Sergeant the reason I was there, and asked to see someone who would listen to what I had to say. Eventually he relented and phoned someone to come through.

After about fifteen minutes, a neatly dressed, tall beanpole of a man with jet-black, slicked back hair appeared. "Mr Grice?" he said, thrusting a bony hand into mine. "Detective Constable Clarke, would you follow me please?"

I followed him along a maze of corridors and into a huge room divided into several well lit glass panelled offices. I was surprised, I had expected to be marched off to some dingy windowless interview room. We entered one of the offices where he pointed to a comfortable looking seat by a large desk.

He picked up the phone. "I am going to have a coffee, Mr Grice would you like one?" I gratefully accepted. He settled into an armchair on the opposite side of the desk and opened up a writing pad. He proceeded to take down my details. You know the form. Name, age, address, married, children, and so on. Eventually he got around to asking me what it was I was here for.

"It's about what happened at the Sandford Valley mine twelve months ago," I began. "Do you know the story I'm referring to?"

"Refresh my memory, Mr Grice."

I love the way these people refuse to commit themselves to a straightforward answer. "Well, I have only been here about six months, so I don't know the full details of exactly what happened, only what I have read in the local newspaper. The story is, four people descended underground at the Sandford Valley mine. They went down in the cage but never came up again. I believe The whole mine was searched but they were never found."

The detective studied me for a moment. "Yes, apparently that is what happened, and it's a mystery which up to date has not been solved. Have you some information that will shed any light on their disappearance?"

I swallowed hard. What on earth was I going to say now? How was I going to convince him of my belief? There was only one way, and that was to come straight out with it. "They are alive," I blurted out. There was no reaction from him. Not a flicker of emotion, not even a look of disbelief.

"What makes you say that Mr Grice? May I call you Peter?"

"Please do," I answered. "I've met them. All four of them."

"Now let me get this right, Peter. You say you have met these men who disappeared that day at the Sandford Valley mine?"

"That is correct."

"I see, and where and when was this?"

"At Harley House. I met Greg at first and then the others last week."

"How did you come to meet them?"

"I live quite close by, and I was walking past the house one Sunday when I saw Greg was in the yard repairing a motorcycle."

This man would have made a superb poker player. His expression never altered. There was no way of telling if he believed me or not. "This Greg you are referring to, is the Greg Baker that disappeared is it?"

"Yes," I replied. "The very same."

"I see, and you say you have met all four of them?"

"Yes."

"Can you describe these gentlemen?" I gave a good description of all four of them. Their faces are locked in my brain. He suddenly sprang out of his chair and opened a draw of a metal filing cabinet. He dropped a pile of photographs onto the desk in front of me. "Are any of those men you saw among these photographs?" I waded through the pile and picked out the four, naming them as I did so. "When did you last see them?"

"Easter Sunday."

"What did they talk about?"

"They made up some fantastic story, which isn't worth repeating, hoping I would swallow it."

"What story?"

"It doesn't matter about the story. It was all a load of nonsense anyway. What interested me most, was they wanted me to contact a man by the name of Charlie Maple."

"Charles Maple? You mean the Manager of the mine?"

"Yes, that's the man."

"They wanted me to tell him to organise a search in the Old Manning's drift area at Hays Heath. They gave me an envelope to give to him with the exact location of where to look."

"To look for what? Did they say what was down there?"

"No, I did ask but they wouldn't tell me."

"Do you have this envelope?"

I felt my face colour up. "No, I appear to have lost it."

"Mmm," he uttered, staring at me for a few seconds. "Well, it's a fascinating story , Peter, but you are forgetting one thing."

"Oh, and what is that?"

"We know for a fact, that these four never made it back to the surface. After taking them down, the cage never returned to the top, so how do you account for the fact that you think they are the ones in that derelict house?"

We looked at each other for a moment. I was trying to figure out what he was thinking, and if he thought I was a bit of a fruitcake.

"Can I ask a question?" I said.

"Be my guest."

"Did you actually see them enter the cage that day?"

The D.C. stared at me for a minute. "Of course not, I wasn't there was I? I had no reason to be. But the manager himself was there. He witnessed them step into the cage and descend."

"Were there any other witnesses?"

"There were none as far as I know. The Manager made a statement at the time that he witnessed them descending in the cage. We also have a statement from the man in the winding house which states the cage never returned to the surface until the alarm was raised, and which was observed to be empty by several members of the rescue team. Why would they lie about that?"

"Well, this only a theory mind, but I think they are all mixed up in some big job. I thought a big haul of drugs or something like that. What better place to hide it than in the abandoned workings of a coal mine while production was halted for the Easter weekend for maintenance.

"Let me stop you there, Peter. You are saying, these four men are involved in some big job and have hidden their ill-gotten gains underground at Hays Heath?"

"Yes that is what I am saying."

"But I repeat, they went down the Sandford Valley mine and there is no way through to Hays Heath."

"But did they go down Sandford Valley? We only have Charlie Maple's word for it. As the manager of both mines, if he's in on this job, it would very easy to organise the whole operation."

The detective sat back in his chair crossing over his legs and twiddling his pen round his finger. He gave me an 'I suppose I had better hear it' looks. "Go on."

"They made sure they were seen on the way to the cage house at Sandford Valley, but never entered the cage. Charlie would have then signalled for the empty cage to be lowered to the bottom."

"Just hold it there, Peter. There's a flaw in your theory here. I happen to know those cages have a weight sensor. They know exactly how many men have entered it. So if nobody entered the cage, the cage operator would know."

"Then he must be in on it," I fired back.

"Ok, let's assume the cage operator is in on it. Please carry on."

"Well, after the cage was sent down, the four would be smuggled out of Sandford Valley and make their way to Hays Heath, where someone would be waiting to organise the cage drop with whatever it is they had. It's still there waiting for them to find a way of bringing it up."

"Mmm, an interesting theory, but if, as you say, Charles Maple is involved, he could have organised the removal himself without them knowing. In fact he may have already done it."

"You are forgetting one thing. He doesn't know the exact whereabouts of the goods. I should imagine that old mine is riddled with tunnels."

"Why do you think they picked on you to make contact?"

"They couldn't break cover themselves could they? They had to wait until a complete stranger came along, someone who wouldn't recognise them. They couldn't very well pick on a local because they would have been rumbled straight away. They obviously think the time is right to make a move."

The detective rose to his feet. "It's a fascinating story, Peter. But it's a bit far-fetched. I want you to go home and forget all about this, and forget about these theories you have come up with. I must warn you not to repeat them to anyone. If you go around accusing Mr Maple of being involved in illegal dealings, you may find yourself in serious trouble. Now I want you to forget you ever came here, do you understand, Peter? Just go home and carry on with your life as normal."

I wasn't exactly surprised he found my story a bit hard to swallow, but I was shocked and a little hurt he had dismissed it in such a way. Not even a thank you, we will let you know. He wasn't even going to think about it. There was nothing I could do. He had blanked me and that was that.

It was back to work the following week, so I had more on my mind than Harley House and the goings on, although it never left my mind completely. I still thought I was right in my theories, but there was no point in dwelling on it now.

About two weeks later while at work, I received a telephone call from D. C. Clarke the detective who had interviewed me at the police station. He wanted me to come and see him as soon as I could. I made arrangements for lunch time. I couldn't think what it was about. I had kept my promise not to repeat anything I had said at the police station that day. I had told Jane of course and wondered if she had said something to someone? I dismissed that thought from my mind. Jane wouldn't have thought any more about it. She wouldn't now have the slightest interest in me or my theories anymore.

I was met at the desk by D.C. Clarke who whisked me to that same room as before. A cup of coffee followed. "I haven't said anything to anyone," I protested. "I promised you I wouldn't and I haven't."

The detective's face broke into a grin. "Calm down, Peter. I know you have kept your promise."

"Then what?"

"The fact is, I found that theory of yours very interesting."

"But you dismissed it out of hand."

"That's what I wanted you to think. If you had been correct in your assumptions and you had broadcast them, it might have jeopardised my inquiries."

"So I was right then?"

"Not exactly."

"What then?"

"I thought about your theory when you left and thought you might have been on to something, so I did some checking around. You see, in January last year, customs discovered a large shipment of drugs hidden in a warehouse at Langshore docks. They lay in wait for weeks waiting for someone to return for it. One night an adjacent warehouse caught fire. We know now it was started deliberately, and in the confusion, the shipment of drugs disappeared from under the noses of the customs officials and was never traced. Your theory about these four with Charles Maple at the helm fitted perfectly as to where those drugs could have been hidden. I honestly thought I had come up trumps, and Hays Heath was where the drugs had been stashed.

Three days ago, I got the ball rolling and insisted on a search team to go down Hays Heath mine and make a thorough search of the Manning's Drift area you mentioned. Mr Maple couldn't understand why I had insisted on a search party from another district when they had one of their own, but I had to work on the theory that the Hays Heath rescue team could have been involved in the drugs haul. I had to concede though, that the local safety officer had to accompany them to guide them to Manning's drift.

Nearly four hours later the double decked cage appeared with the top deck stopping at ground level. Four rescue workers stepped out carrying two stretchers. Then the cage then rose to let the men out of the bottom section. Two more stretchers followed.

"Better look at these," said one of the stretcher bearers to me. He indicated to the others to remove the sheets. We all stood there open mouthed as four skeletons were uncovered.

"They were just lying there together at the top of Manning's drift like they were sleeping," said one of the bearers.

The detective looked at me. "Do I need to tell you who they were, Peter."

I could feel the blood draining from my face. "They are the four that disappeared aren't they?"

He nodded. "Yes they are. Forensics confirmed it was definitely them. How they got from Sandford Valley to Hays Heath is a complete mystery, and is likely to remain so. A complete search of both mines in the adjoining areas revealed there is no way through. It had been assumed they were overcome by blackdamp, but the search party says there were no signs of it. The manager is in complete shock. He insists he watched them descend in the cage that morning. As for you, Peter, I don't know how to explain your experience. You will probably never know how or why it happened, but it looks as though it happened for a purpose."

"I can't explain it," I said. "I've had some experiences in my time but this is the weirdest one I have ever had. I know some people claim to be subject to these weird happenings like this one, but not me. I don't really believe in anything like this. To be honest it has unnerved me a little. I think I shall be wary of going to sleep for some while."

The detective rose from his seat and shook my hand. "Just reassure yourself it was perhaps pure coincidence. I'm sure it won't be long before you put it to the back of your mind."

I spent the rest of the afternoon busying myself trying to do just that. I gave a lot of thought to what the detective had said about it being nothing more than coincidence. I'm sure he thought, like Charlie Maple, I had read about it somewhere and I dreamt it all while it was on my mind, which wasn't true of course. I had definitely met those four men.

The whole thing had unnerved me, but I suppose the fact that I knew I wasn't cracking up gave me some comfort and eased my nervousness, but I don't think I would ever forget it. I certainly didn't want any more experiences like that.

I returned home that night after work with my brain in a whirl. I thought about ringing Jane to tell her about my experience, but I decided she wouldn't be interested. She had after all given me an ultimatum about giving up this job or not. If she didn't hear from me in two days she would presume I was staying here and that the marriage would be over. I hate ultimatums and wasn't going to be bullied into anything, so stubbornly I didn't ring and neither did she, so I had to presume it was now all over between us.

As I slid off my jacket my pen fell from my pocket and rolled behind the radiator. As I bent down to pick it up I saw that elusive envelope. I opened it up and pulled out a map of Hays Heath with reference to Manning's Drift and an x marking a certain spot. It was signed by Bill. "It was no dream then," I said to myself. I really did meet those men. I suddenly had a compulsion to go to Harley House. I put on my warm overcoat and headed down the lane. I had a sudden urge to return Bill's letter to the house.

I must have stood a good fifteen minutes at the gate staring at that unloved looking building. I eventually made my way to the kitchen door to find it slightly ajar. I nudged it open. The hinges creaked and groaned before it came to rest. I stood in the doorway looking into the gloomy interior before stepping inside. The stench of blocked up drains and rotting wood filled my nostrils. I made my way through the kitchen to the living room, my shoes crunching the dirt underfoot. The living room was the same scene

I had viewed on my previous visit, but with probably a few more cobwebs and an added layer of dust. I removed the map from the envelope and spread it out on the table. I wrote on it 'JOB DONE.' and placed it on the table, propping it up against an old oil lamp. As I stood looking at it, wondering why on earth I was doing such an idiotic thing, I sensed a presence behind me. I whirled around to see a grey haired man dressed in a smart grey suit standing in the living room doorway. Although my heart was palpitating, I wasn't frightened by his presence; there was an aura of calm radiating from him. I recognised him straight away from the descriptions the four had mentioned. It was the operator. "What are you doing here?" I asked.

"I'm here on behalf of your friends to thank you for what you have done. Now thanks to you, their bodies have been recovered and given a proper burial, which has allowed them to make a fresh start."

"But I didn't believe them," I said. "I thought they were all crooks. It was pure coincidence I went to the police."

A faint smile appeared on the operators face. "No, it wasn't a coincidence, Peter. It was planted in your mind to inform the police. You see, if your friends had told you about their bodies lying undiscovered in the mine, you would have walked away thinking they were completely mad. I made you suspicious of their motives, and once you were convinced they were up to something illegal, I planted the idea in your head of convincing the police to make a search of the mine."

"So I was being controlled all the time?"

"Yes, I'm sorry, you were, but it was for the good of your friends."

"It wasn't Greg who selected me for this task was it? It was you, wasn't it?"

"Yes it was," he replied.

"But why me?" I asked.

"Because you also have begun to tread the wrong direction in your life, Peter. Would you like me to show you what is in store for you if you don't correct it?"

I felt sick. I knew straight away he was referring to my obsession with my career and money to the detriment of my family life. He obviously felt it serious enough to warrant an intervention. I swallowed hard as I remembered the horrific results shown to the others if they had continued as they were. I was sure the operator would show me I was heading for a similar fate if I didn't do something about it. "You have no need to show me," I gasped. "I know where I went wrong and I promise I will put it right immediately."

The operator gave me a long lingering stare as if weighing up my answer. His image began to slowly disappear, issuing this warning as his image faded. "Very well, Peter, but I warn you of the consequences if you fail to carry out your promise. It means, YOU AND I WILL BE SEEING EACH OTHER AGAIN, AT MY PLACE."

THE END

About Fred Maddox

Fred was born in Stoke-on-Trent in 1941 during the bleak times of the war years. His father was a coal miner and his mother worked in the pottery industry. Stoke was a bleak place in those days. Money and jobs were hard to come by, but Fred received a good standard grammar school education. Favourite subjects. English, Art and Science. On leaving school at the age of 15, Fred gained employment as an apprentice motor engineer, gaining his City and Guilds. He later became a Regional Manager for a national motor components distributor.

As a young child, Fred wrote stories and related them to anyone who would listen.

In 2003 at the age of 62 Fred suffered a mild heart attack prompting him to take early retirement, emigrating to Cyprus, where he decided to take up his writing seriously. To date, Fred has had three novels published.

Other Book(s) by Fred Maddox

Deadlier Than The Male, ISBN 9781905809547

Peter Milton had always promised himself he would never again live in poverty, as he had done as a child. That promise became an obsession, so great, it took over his life.

A Genuine Fake, ISBN 9781905809929

Tracy's father died from the tremendous stress of trying to keep his antique business afloat. She takes over his business and soon realised what her father had been up against. She formulates a plan for retribution. Her plan worked beyond all expectations. The money bug had now bitten, she wants more, but can she get away with it?

JOSS, ISBN 9781907728327

Joss Hinchcliff was at a disadvantage from the moment he was born. He lived a hard life but one day he found an abandoned vintage car which he re-built, it was no ordinary car. Whilst out on a road test one day, it whisked him away to a mysterious place which would change his life forever.

Lightning Source UK Ltd.
Milton Keynes UK
UKOW04f1836100913

216949UK00001B/23/P